Entwined Publishing books by Peter E. Fenton

Single Books
The Woodcarver's Model

The Declan Hunt Mysteries
Mann Hunt
Hoodoo House
The Burnt

I0527535

The Declan Hunt Mysteries

THE BURNT

PETER E. FENTON

ENTWINED PUBLISHING

The Burnt
ISBN # 978-1-80250-252-7
©Copyright Peter E. Fenton 2025
Cover Art by Erin Dameron-Hill ©Copyright August 2025
Interior text design by Entwined Publishing
Published by Evidence, an Entwined Publishing imprint

Published in 2025 by Entwined Publishing, United Kingdom.

Entwined Publishing is a division of Totally Entwined Group Limited.

THE BURNT

Dedication

This book is dedicated to the people of Jasper, Alberta,
as they recover from the fire of 2024.

Chapter One

Simon Griffin reclined on a large leather chair in the sun room of his home in Banff — a home that had been unimaginatively called Mountainview by its original owners. After he'd purchased it, Simon had renamed the house The Paddock as a tribute to his favourite bar in Toronto, the city he'd grown up in.

He never tired of the view from this vantage point, especially in the evening as the sun dipped behind Sundance Ridge, which spread out before him beyond the Bow River. The mountains carried a heavy coat of white January snow that slowly faded out of view as the darkness enveloped the surrounding property. It was six-thirty in the evening. The only light visible now was from the backyard lamps which flooded the property as a security measure against intruders and sightseers who wanted to get a look at Simon's famous house.

Simon was proud that The Paddock was one of the largest private properties within the confines of the town of Banff — a property which lay within the national park boundary. When he'd bought it, he had wanted a place away from the hustle and bustle of the city. It was ridiculously big for his needs — over seven hundred and fifty square metres in size with six bedrooms and seven bathrooms. He had joked about having one bathroom for every day of the week. His friends had said he was nuts to leave the faster pace of the big city.

"Visiting Banff on a holiday, sure, but who actually lives there other than the kids who wait tables at the tourist restaurants?"

If Simon wanted big-city life, Calgary was only an hour away. He kept an apartment there in case he was in town late for business, but for the most part he liked Banff...except for the tourists. When he had moved here in 1984, it wasn't so bad. Back then he'd been able to keep the gates to his driveway open and walk about the streets without having to dodge around people. But in recent years, things had gotten out of control, and now, during the summer, they even closed down Banff Avenue to cars in an attempt to control the flow of visitors. Ironically, thanks to its natural beauty and wide-open spaces, Banff was now overpopulated with tourists. They walked blindly out into the streets. Some even parked their cars in front of his driveway — *"It's okay, I'll only be a minute."* Simon sometimes didn't want to leave his property due to the swarms of picture-snapping sightseers.

Through the window, Simon spotted a young man playing with the latch on the back gate — another tourist caught out too late while snowshoeing along the well-worn trail which ran between the property and the Bow River. The man was persistent, rattling away at the gate latch.

Simon went to the back door and opened it.

"This is private property," he called out, trying not to sound annoyed. "The gate's locked. You'll have to keep going along the river 'til you come to the street." He waved the man in the right direction.

"Sorry," the fellow yelled back. "Nice place. I thought this was my hotel." The man shrugged and headed off in the wrong direction.

Idiot.

Once he was sure the man was gone, Simon headed back and flopped into his chair. If he had any real clout in this town, he'd have that damned pathway fenced off and the tourists would stop disturbing his peace.

His thoughts were interrupted as Jasmine, his housekeeper, brought him his after-dinner coffee.

He glanced up at her. Her shoulder-length wavy brown hair, rounded face and tall, slender frame were more familiar to him than his own features. She gave him a weak smile. Her glazed eyes and furrowed brow signalled to him that she was working through one of her migraines.

"Thank you, my dear," he said. "Why don't you just call it a day and go and rest that head?"

She gently rubbed her temples. "Thank you, sir. I'll be fine."

Although Jasmine worked for him, she was the closest thing Simon had to family... aside from his son.

"By the way, a boy dropped this off for you this afternoon," she said, pulling out an envelope from her left pants pocket. "I would have given it to you earlier, but you had the office door closed, and I needed to lie down."

Simon didn't remember hearing a car on the drive, and a visitor would have had to buzz through on the intercom to gain access.

"A boy dropped it off?"

"That's what I said."

"At the front door?"

"Yes, sir."

"But, Jasmine, the gates are locked. How did he get in to knock on the front door?"

She shrugged. "Maybe he climbed the fence."

She turned and left him with the envelope. Just as she was closing the door she added, "He said someone asked him to deliver it." Then she was gone.

Simon looked at the envelope in his hands. He turned it over and examined the back. Nothing. No identifiers. He opened the envelope. Inside he found a single letter-size piece of white paper with a simple hand-written message on it.

I'm watching you and I know what you did.

Simon's hands began to shake when he saw the signature.

Milo.

* * * *

Simon pondered the letter all night. He wanted a second opinion, so he set up a walk with someone he trusted. Before he went out, he bundled up like he was preparing himself for a polar expedition. Icy temperatures in Banff were a winter certainty, but that didn't mean he had to be uncomfortable. It was first thing in the morning and the cold hadn't been tempered by the sun.

As he trudged along the frost-covered river walk, he said a brusque "Good morning" to each crack-of-dawn cross-country skier and snowshoer he came across. His companion, Tom Semple, frowned. In contrast to Simon, Tom dressed like he was going out for dinner at a high-end restaurant, sporting a camelhair coat with a tasteful scarf, brown gloves and shoes, and a fedora. His only concession to the cold was a pair of earmuffs.

"It's damned cold out here and you have a gym in your house. If you're trying to stay fit, you could be using that, instead of making us both freeze out here."

"Fresh air, my old friend, is the key to a long and healthy life. Besides, I wanted to talk to you and be sure Jasmine didn't hear us."

"Oh?"

They trudged on for another ten metres before Simon reached into his pocket and pulled out a folded piece of paper. He handed it to Tom.

"This arrived yesterday. It was hand-delivered by a kid who clambered over the fence. He said he was told to give it to someone in the house. Jasmine received it and gave it to me."

Tom read it.

I'm watching you and I know what you did.
Milo.

The colour in Tom's cheeks paled slightly. He turned the paper over to check the back, then held it up to the light of the sun. "Do you think it's some sort of joke? We had the best people in the company look for him, and…nothing."

"Why would someone do this?" Simon asked.

"There are a lot of sick bastards out there."

Simon shook his head. "Why hand-deliver it and not mail it?"

"They wanted to make sure it got to you. Nobody trusts the mail anymore."

Simon frowned. "It can't be just to pick at an old scab. Whoever sent this must want something. But what? They haven't made a request for money...yet."

Simon stared at Tom for a moment before he asked the question foremost on his mind. "Could it really be from Milo?"

Tom pursed his lips. "I don't know."

They walked in silence until they reached the gate to Simon's backyard. Tom turned to him. "You know I busted my ass looking for him when he left — my whole team did."

"I know you did."

Tom shrugged. "Look, I have an idea. Maybe we just need an outside perspective on this."

"Meaning?"

"I briefly met this guy last year at a function at the Palliser Hotel. He's a private investigator based in Calgary. He specialises in cases requiring...discretion. I looked into the guy. From what I hear, he's reliable, fearless and they say he can really take a punch."

"You looked into the guy?" Simon smiled. "Sounds more like you've got a crush on him."

"The point is," Tom said, "maybe he could help."

Simon raised an eyebrow. "I assume you already have this miracle-worker's contact information?"

Tom rifled through his wallet, pulled out a creased business card and handed it to Simon. The card read *Declan Hunt Investigations*.

Simon stuffed it into his pocket.

"All right. I'll call him. And maybe if you're lucky, he'll want to interrogate you...personally." Simon cocked his head. "You all right, Tom? You don't look like you've slept in a while."

"Sleep's for people who have nothing better to do with their all-too-short lives," Tom snapped.

As they approached the house, Simon said, "I guess you've heard the rumours that Harlen Feist is in hospital. Pancreatic cancer, I hear."

Tom nodded. "He probably won't last long."

"No."

"I guess the company will be looking for his replacement," Tom added.

"I suppose so."

"Simon, you know you're the obvious one for the job, don't you?"

Simon turned to Tom. "All the more reason to clear up this Milo letter business. And fast."

Chapter Two

Charlie Watts sat at his desk in the front room of Declan Hunt Investigations. He'd spent the last few hours trying to find information on a guy named Tyler Chipping. It wasn't that there hadn't been anything to find. His social media accounts were overflowing with images of Tyler out dancing, Tyler out drinking, Tyler out at restaurants. Some of them were Tyler alone, but most were of him in the company of attractive men. Not unusual for a young gay male. What was unusual was that he appeared to have no followers. Either nobody was particularly interested in him, or he had intentionally adjusted his privacy settings so that others could view his photos, but couldn't comment or follow.

Declan Hunt Investigations had been hired to find anything on Chipping that could support his company in firing him. Management were of the opinion that Chipping was, in their words, a waste of corporate space. Declan had given Charlie the job – his first solo case as a private investigator in training. Charlie was using the tool he was best at wielding — the computer — yet he could find nothing of value. Point scored — Tyler Chipping. Charlie was batting zero, and he wasn't happy about it. His ego was taking it personally.

Charlie glanced down at his desk, spotting the box of business cards that had just arrived from the printers. He picked up one of the cards. It was crisp, white, and bore the name and logo of "Declan Hunt Investigations". Embossed in black below, it identified the cardholder as —

Charlie Watts, Researcher.

Charlie had come up with the job title himself, and Declan had approved it. It was too soon to print cards that said "Private Investigator" since Charlie was only in training, but it carried more clout than his previous title of "Office Manager."

"Researcher. Yeah, right," he muttered as he flipped the card away from him. It gracefully sailed across the room and landed at the feet of his boss.

"How goes the hunt for Mr Chipping?" Declan asked, propping himself on Charlie's desk.

"Fine, if we're looking to find out what he ate for dinner on his birthday," Charlie answered, then looked up. "Which was steak, medium rare, mashed potatoes with sour cream and a side of roasted cauliflower. Care to know what he ate for dessert?"

Declan smiled. "Part of my brain is telling me to ask if you found anything pertinent to the case, but the rest of my body is telling me to keep my mouth shut."

"Smart body."

Declan nodded. "The standard searches yielded nothing, right?"

"Nothing that could pertain to his employment. It's almost like he doesn't work."

"That's what his employer is saying."

Declan walked around to Charlie's side of the desk.

Charlie sighed. *Why does Declan always look perfect? It's like every piece of off-the-rack clothing was made specifically for his body.*

Charlie was wearing his best long-sleeved dress shirt and khakis and still looked like he'd either slept in them or stolen them from a charity bin.

Declan leaned over and kissed him on the top of the head. "I think the time has come for you to earn your stripes as a real gumshoe."

"What do you mean by that?"

"Not all problems can be solved at a computer, although you've done things with this machine that amaze me to this day. As scary as it might sound, sometimes you have to hit the pavement and ask your questions in person."

"As I recall, I did that when I first started here and almost got myself killed."

Declan nodded. "Yeah, but in this case you'll be talking to people from a human resources firm, not the mob. You just have to make sure you don't let Tyler Chipping know you're there. That's where all this research you've done will come in handy," he said, patting Charlie on the shoulder. "You know exactly what he looks like."

* * * *

Charlie stood in front of Chapman, Sherbrook and Finch, the small human resources firm Tyler Chipping was working at...for now. Charlie's nerves were on edge. He didn't want to let Declan down. His computer research hadn't been completely in vain. He had identified two employees who seemed to be the office gossips based on the contents of their social media posts. Maybe he'd get lucky.

He stood and waited on the street. The winter sun was low in the sky and shining directly into his eyes. It was twenty below with a wind chill that made it feel closer to minus thirty. He loved Calgary. He just hated winter. Why couldn't this be happening in July?

Charlie checked his phone and huddled against the building.

A few minutes after noon, two young women exited from the main door of the one-storey office building. They were chatting wildly to each other. As they neared Charlie, he moved into their path.

"Excuse me. Sorry to bother you, but do you work here?"

"Yes," one said, hesitantly. She peered at Charlie through the fur of her hooded parka. She was mummified against the cold, the part of her face not shielded by her coat was covered by a scarf and sunglasses.

Smarter than me.

"My name's Charlie Watts."

He pulled out the small metal business card case that his friend Carrie had given him when he started working for Declan. His hands shook a bit as he opened it. The case had a tight catch on it and when he finally got the lid to pop open, several of the cards spilled onto the ground. Most of them blew away in the wind, but Charlie managed to bend over and retrieve a card that was stuck to his boot. The day was going from bad to worse.

Charlie handed it to the mummified woman.

The woman looked at the card and read, in a whispery voice, "Declan Hunt Investigations. Charlie Watts, Researcher." She lowered her glasses and stared him directly in the eyes. "*You're* a private detective?"

This was not going well. Charlie swallowed and stared back at her. "Look, I was just wondering if you'd be able to answer a few questions for me. My firm has been hired to do a background check on Tyler Chipping. Do you work with him?"

The term 'background check' was an exaggeration Charlie came up with to hide his real purpose.

"Well," the other woman said, "I'm not sure we should be talking about this here."

Charlie considered his options. "Would you be more comfortable talking over lunch? My treat."

The first woman said, "Maybe it would be all right, if we get to pick the place."

"Sure," he replied.

The two looked at each other, simultaneously spun back to Charlie, and shouted "Bastion's!"

Charlie assumed Bastion's was an expensive restaurant based on their enthusiastic reaction to being taken to lunch. *Hopefully not too expensive.*

The women led Charlie along the street for a few blocks then steered him down a back alley and through a door into a small café. They made their way to a booth in the darkest corner near the back and stripped off their polar-wear. One of the women was a redhead whose scarlet lipstick matched the colour of her thick mane of hair. The other, a blonde, was more reserved with her makeup, with a light blush on her cheeks and pale lipstick. Both were in their early twenties. As they sat down, he pieced together why they had recommended the place. The waiter was tall, had raven-black hair, blue eyes and the perkiest butt

Charlie had ever seen. He quickly came over to take their orders.

"Crystal. Laura and...friend," he said, smiling at Charlie. "I'm Carrick. I'll be your server this afternoon. Will it be the usual for you ladies?" he asked in a spine-melting Irish accent.

They giggled out a "Yes."

"And for you, sir?" he asked, with a sexy emphasis on 'sir', even though he appeared to be Charlie's age.

"I'll have...whatever they're having."

"Excellent choice, sir," Carrick said before he smiled broadly at Charlie, turned on his toes and walked away.

"Hey," Crystal, the redhead, said as she swatted Charlie on the arm. "You leave him alone. He's ours."

"I'm not so sure about that now," the other woman, who he now knew was Laura, added.

Charlie was thoroughly enjoying his time with Crystal and Laura. They adopted him like a long-lost friend and soon they were engaged in conversation which slowly turned to Tyler Chipping.

"Declan Hunt Investigations has been hired by Chapman, Sherbrook and Finch's law firm to look into Tyler," Charlie started.

"Is he going to be fired?" Crystal asked. She seemed quite excited at the prospect.

"I didn't say that," Charlie replied. "They're just assessing his performance and want to make sure that his work...conforms to the corporation's mandate," *before they fire him*, he added to himself. "Because Mr Chipping's openly gay, they wanted to make sure that if anything negative came out of our investigations, it couldn't be interpreted as homophobia on their part."

"And you can do that how?" Laura asked.

"Both Declan and I are gay and the firm is known for handling cases like this…in an unbiased way."

Crystal looked around then whispered, "Gay's the *last* thing that guy's got to worry about."

As lunch progressed, they opened up to Charlie with all of the lurid details of Chipping's corporate abuses. It was clear that they didn't like Tyler.

"I honestly don't know how he's kept his job this long," Laura said as they departed Bastion's. She took Charlie's card and wrote a number on the back. "This is a friend of mine who works in the company's accounting department. Farzan will give you everything you need to know. He's pissed at Tyler. Farzan got him his job. Now he feels *his* reputation's in the sewer because of what Tyler's been up to."

Crystal gave Charlie a hug and kissed him on the cheek. "Now, my advice to you is to get back in there and get Carrick's number. You obviously have a better chance than the two of us." She giggled and the two women walked away, leaving Charlie alone in the cold sunshine.

Chapter Three

Charlie mounted the stairs to the office. It was five o'clock and he was running late. He pulled out his phone and sent a quick text to Carrie.

Declan and I will be there by seven. I have to deal with a few things then I'll come home.

Home. Charlie had only had two places in his life that he'd considered home. The first was the one he'd shared with his parents and grandmother. The second was the apartment he now shared with his best friend Carrie, who had taken him in when he'd been kicked out of his parents' place. Now he stood one floor below the home he wished he had — the apartment above the office, where Declan lived.

Living with Declan would be the last home he could hope for, but they both had to be ready for that. Working and living together was a big step.

Crash.

The ceiling trembled. Charlie shook his head. He really had to buy Declan a thicker weight mat to muffle the noise.

Crash.

A text came in from Carrie.

Looking forward to seeing Declan.

Carrie had been bugging Charlie for weeks about getting together with Declan for dinner. But something had always gotten in the way. Tonight, he had to make it happen.

Charlie ran to his desk and typed as quickly as his fingers would allow. Forty-five minutes later, he printed a copy of the report of his interviews to pass on to Declan. As Charlie shut down his computer for the night, the detective walked into the reception area.

"Still working?" he asked Charlie.

"Just documenting my progress on the case," Charlie answered. "I cornered some of Tyler Chipping's coworkers. They were more than willing to help out. I hope it's okay—I treated them to lunch. That can't be interpreted as me bribing them, can it?"

Declan laughed. "No. I think you'll be safe."

"Their names are all in the report. They were happy to slag the guy. They even gave me contact info for another guy named Farzan who corroborated their stories. I talked to him this afternoon. He referred to Tyler as"—Charlie looked at his report—"and I quote, 'a backstabbing bastard'. Apparently, everyone thinks Mr Chipping is an obnoxious slacker who rarely does anything at work except live on Grindr. Among other things, he was caught by one of his coworkers banging a guy in the office of a VP who was on vacation. I don't think a wrongful dismissal due to sexual orientation is at play here. The company should be able to fire him safely."

Charlie looked up from his notes. "I was trying to use only publicly accessible sources but, just to be sure, when I got back here to the office, I hacked into his work computer. I was surprised they had such poor security. Anyway, I found almost nothing that appeared work-related. There was a ton of really hot porn which was downloaded after hours during the time he was billing a client for working overtime—I cross-referenced the download times with his work-time log. The guy is basically an idiot."

Charlie hesitated before continuing. "What's creepy, to me at least, is that he also had a computer folder labelled 'Hunt'. Chipping's got a ton of info on you, photos saved from news sites and copies of stories about the Ian Mann case."

"You think he's a crazy stalker?"

Charlie scowled. "That thought had crossed my mind."

Declan shrugged. "As long as none of the photos were taken by him personally, I don't think we have to worry about it."

Charlie didn't like the idea that a total stranger was fantasising about his boss...and boyfriend.

Declan glanced down at him and smirked. "I don't want to sound like a self-absorbed asshole, but that sort of thing does happen on occasion."

Charlie looked at the gorgeous guy. "Of course it does."

There was a moment of silence before Declan said, "Don't worry. I've got you, and that's all I need."

Charlie's heart beat a little faster. He smiled and handed Declan the file. "So, I guess once you've reviewed this, we can send it off to the lawyers and let them deal with it?"

"Yes. Good work, Charlie. I'll look at this now before we head out for dinner."

Charlie watched Declan slowly walk back to his office.

Everything that man does is sexy.

Charlie stared at the stacks of mail, reports, photographs and statements which had all migrated from what had been neat piles into one inbreeding mass on his desk. There wasn't even room for him to put a coffee – if he had one, which he desperately needed if he was going to make it through the evening. He went into the kitchen and made a latte, then sat back at his desk and placed it on the only clear surface – the floor.

Charlie looked at the pile of paperwork and put his hands on his head.

Where do I even begin?

Ever since he'd started working at Declan Hunt Investigations, business had increased. Declan had given the credit to him. Charlie knew better. It was just pure, dumb luck. That, and the high-profile cases they had been lucky enough to take on. Something had happened to the firm's public image. When Charlie had first started working here, any mention of Declan in the press was accompanied by a stock picture of his ripped, soot-covered torso as he'd pulled a man from a burning car during a well-reported case. That image attracted clientele from the gay male and straight female community. Lately, however, there had been more images of the two of them. Granted, Charlie had been relegated to the role of 'cute companion', but Charlie liked the attention.

Then things had started to devolve. Since Charlie had begun working toward gaining his private investigator's licence, little things had been falling through the cracks. Calls weren't being returned in a timely manner, invoices weren't being sent out promptly and paperwork wasn't being submitted to their accountant, Mr Attwal. He had dropped by just yesterday to find out if he should remove them from his client roster since he hadn't heard from anyone in a while. Declan had told Charlie not to worry about it. He'd said that these were just growing pains as Charlie transitioned into work in the field. Charlie wasn't so sure.

Declan stepped out of his office and said, "Should we be heading out soon?"

As Charlie spun around to reply, he kicked over his coffee.

"God damn it!" he shouted as he dropped to the floor and began to mop up the mess with what he realised was an outgoing invoice. "Shit!"

"Hey, it's okay," Declan said. "It's nothing that can't be reprinted."

"That's *not* the point!"

Declan came back from the kitchenette with a wad of paper towels. He joined Charlie on the floor and helped him sop up the coffee.

"There. All better," Declan said.

Charlie muttered, "Not better."

Declan gently took a hold of Charlie by the shoulders. "Okay. What's wrong?"

"Just look," Charlie said motioning to his desk. He fought back tears. "Between my coursework and taking on my own cases, I haven't been doing my job. Nothing is getting done. If I don't get invoices out, we won't have any money coming in, and bills won't get paid. We'll end up on the street."

"I don't think that's going to—"

"No!" Charlie snapped. "I'm not doing the company any favours working like this."

"You're right," Declan said. "You can't do all the admin work when you're working on cases."

Charlie crossed his arms. "I don't know what to do."

Declan stood up. "I do. I think you're going to have to find us a new office manager—"

"No," Charlie interrupted weakly.

"—so you can focus on the cases. Let's call it a day. You can start fresh tomorrow morning and clear up any paperwork you can, then get an ad out there. Your next case, Mr Watts, is to find us an office manager. Just not one as cute as you. And while you're at it, why don't you set up a new workspace for yourself?"

"Where?" Charlie asked, looking around.

"You could set a desk up over there," Declan said, indicating the area just outside his door. "You'd be facing out toward the main room. That would give you privacy and let you keep an eye on whatever's happening. You'd have space for a bookcase and filing cabinets behind you along the wall. During the day there's plenty of natural light."

Charlie felt a rush of excitement.

Declan continued. "And then, when the bank accounts are a little healthier, we can have someone throw up a wall with a door. I can see the name plate on it—Charlie Watts, Private Investigator."

"You mean it? Really?"

"You bet. You'll need privacy."

Charlie lunged at Declan, throwing his arms around him, toppling them both back to the floor. The moment was interrupted by the chirp of the alarm system on the ground-level door. It was a little late for someone to just drop by for a visit. There was the sound of heavy footsteps on the stairs. They both got to their feet and Charlie instinctively slid around behind Declan as the door opened. A large hulk of a man entered the room.

"Sergeant Hunt," Charlie said.

"Dad," Declan said.

Declan took several deep breaths, something Charlie noticed he did whenever his father came through the door.

Something was wrong. The Sarge didn't just drop around for the hell of it. Charlie gently put a hand on Declan's back.

"Declan," the cop started, "you remember Archie Whitcher?"

Charlie could feel the broad muscles in Declan's back tense.

"Freddy Whitcher's father," Declan replied.

"Yeah. Well, I thought you'd want to know that someone killed the son of a bitch late this morning. I got a call from your old partner Gary Sawchuck. He was on the scene."

"Oh."

Declan's voice was emotionless.

"A neighbour called it in. Sawchuck said he'd been beaten, then shot."

Declan said nothing.

"Sawchuck arrived just before Archie took his last breath."

"Thanks for letting me know," Declan said.

"There was one other thing. Just before Archie died, Sawchuck heard him say something that sounded to him like, 'Tell Hunt it was Milo.' That mean anything to you?"

"Nope."

"Anyway, Sawchuck's tied up with the paperwork, so I said I'd let you know. He thought you'd want to hear it in person. If you think of anything, get in touch with him."

The two men stood in silence. Charlie wondered how long this stalemate would last before someone blinked first. It was The Sarge.

"Well, I should get going."

Declan nodded and the sergeant turned, walked out of the office then down the stairs.

Charlie thought of the picture of Freddy Whitcher that Declan kept in his office. He was the kid who had run away from his father's beatings when his dad had found out he was gay.

"Are you okay?" Charlie asked.

"Yup."

Charlie knew Declan wasn't okay. "You think you'll still be up for dinner with Carrie tonight? She's really looking forward to getting to know you better, and it might help take your mind off...things."

Declan finally took his eyes off the door. "I'm gonna have to take a rain check. Besides, I don't think I'll be great company for the two of you. I've got some work I need to take care of."

"If you want me to stick around, I'll reschedule," Charlie offered.

Declan smiled. "No. You two haven't gone out and raised hell for a while. You deserve the break."

"Yeah. Sure."

Charlie leaned over and gave Declan a kiss. "Would you mind if I came back here after dinner and spent the night?"

Declan gave him a weak smile. "That'd be nice," he said, then turned and headed into his office.

Charlie put on his coat and made his way down the stairs. He knew how important this was to Declan, but he wondered if there would ever be a time when life came first and work came second?

Chapter Four

Declan was unsettled by the news his father had delivered.

Archie Whitcher is dead.

He'd never thought he'd see the day when that man would pay for what he'd done to his son. But Archie's last message... *Who the hell is Milo? And why did Archie want me to know about him?*

Maybe Declan could find something in his notes from the last time he'd encountered Archie Whitcher — notes he hadn't looked at for a number of years.

Declan opened the large cupboard in his office that contained the safe. Inside, underneath various boxes and binders, was a file folder labelled *Freddy*. He placed it on his desk, poured himself a scotch, then sat down and opened the file. Declan looked over the photocopies of the pages of his old police notebook.

While Declan and Gary Sawchuck had been the ones who had discovered and dealt with the identification of Freddy's body, the investigation had been turned over to a Sergeant McKeckran. Declan had encountered the homophobic asshole again just last year. McKeckran had tried to close the file on the Ian Mann case because he was sure the victim was gay. Years before, he had swept the Freddy Whitcher death under the same carpet. Declan knew the case had never been adequately investigated.

The rage returned.

There was nothing of value to be found in the notes other than stirring up a painful memory. Declan placed a quick call to Gary Sawchuck. A gruff voice answered on the other end. "Yeah."

"Gary, it's Declan. I got your message. Are you still on the scene?"

"Forensics is wrapping up for the day. We'll be back tomorrow, but the body's gone and we've been through the preliminaries. I'll keep you posted if there's anything else that pertains to you. You got any idea what Archie was talking about when he used your name before he died?"

"Nope," Declan replied. "All right, Gary. Thanks. Keep in touch."

Declan disconnected. He wasn't going to get any sleep tonight unless… He knew what he needed to do next.

Declan got into his van and began to drive toward an address in Forest Lawn. He hadn't been there in over a decade, but certain places he'd never forget.

He thought back to the morning when he and Gary Sawchuck had been on patrol near an industrial park. Declan had seen flames in a vacant lot. His first thought was that it was probably a fire set by some homeless guys trying to keep warm. Winter in Calgary could be unforgiving, especially for those who lived on the streets.

As they got nearer they had discovered that the fire was larger than they'd expected. Still, it wasn't close to any buildings and they'd figured they could put it out with the extinguishers in their cruiser's trunk. No need to involve the Calgary Fire Department.

As the junior, Declan was the one who'd ventured out into the cold while his partner stayed warm inside the car, finishing off his coffee. Sunrise wasn't due for another hour so it was still dark out when Declan had pulled the first of the extinguishers out and tackled the blaze. He'd emptied the contents of one extinguisher, then put out what remained of the fire with the second.

Declan could still remember the rest like it happened yesterday. He had pulled out his flashlight and scanned the area around the fire which appeared to have been fuelled by a bunch of stacked wooden skids. Off to one side of the blaze, under another skid, was a backpack, blackened by smoke but only lightly singed. Declan had opened it and shone his flashlight inside, discovering some clothing. From the size of the shirt he'd pulled out, it appeared to belong to a kid—a teen, probably. He'd dug deeper and found a wallet. There was identification in it—a Calgary Transit Monthly Youth Pass which was just about to expire, and a student card. The name on the card was Freddy Whitcher.

Another runaway was the first thing that had come to Declan's mind. He'd figured the poor kid had probably been frightened away when the fire grew out of control and forgotten to take his pack. Then Declan had seen it—a human leg protruding from under a charred wooden pallet. Inked into the leg was a rough tattoo— 'M+F' surrounded by a heart.

Once the forensics team had taken charge and they had an address for the kid, Declan and Sawchuck had been dispatched to see if anyone there could identify the body. Declan was glad that Gary had taken the lead. He'd knocked on the front door. It was opened by a guy who had clearly been drinking. His hair was unwashed, his face unshaven and his clothes were shabby. He looked like a man who'd given up on life, or life had given up on him. It was Archie Whitcher.

Gary had asked the guy if he had a teenaged son named Freddy, and the guy had asked "What's that little faggot done this time?" Those words were etched in Declan's memory. He had spent his early years having words like that wielded against him by his own father and was sensitive to them being used against this kid.

Archie had claimed his son had left the previous day and hadn't come back. Then Gary had asked if Freddy had a tattoo on one of his legs. Declan remembered Archie replying that it was something Freddy and his faggot friend had done all on their own, then said if Freddy was in trouble, it was *his* problem. Archie had started to shut the door but Gary had blocked it with his foot, and after he'd revealed that they thought Freddy was dead, the tone of the encounter had changed.

Declan was there a day later when Archie was brought in to identify the remains of his son. All he could be shown was what was left of the tattooed boy's lower right leg. Archie had shown no emotion. He'd just said, "That's him," before walking out.

During the investigation, it was discovered that Archie Whitcher had served time in jail for many of the *choices* he'd made in his life, but in Declan's opinion, he'd never paid a price for what had led up to his son's death.

Until now.

* * * *

Declan parked across from Archie Whitcher's house. He stared at the dilapidated bungalow. He pictured what the place would have looked like earlier in the day with squad cars, paramedics and forensics vehicles blocking the road. He imagined bystanders trying to get a look at the victim as he was wheeled away in a body bag. Investigators would have been comparing notes on what they had found and what was said. Now everything was quiet. Police tape surrounded the darkened home, marking it off as an active crime scene. It was the only evidence that something out of the ordinary had happened here. Surprisingly, there didn't even appear to be a manned police cruiser standing guard. Budgets being what they were these days, the force probably couldn't spare a cop and car just to sit there and guard the empty house. Or maybe their priority wasn't the death of a low-level criminal.

No matter what, in the light of the streetlamps, the house looked rundown and drenched in sadness, just as Declan remembered it the last time he'd been there.

Declan parked the van and clenched his teeth. He wanted to get this over with as quickly as possible.

Chapter Five

Charlie had made reservations at a new place in town, a seafood restaurant called *Carp Diem*. He could see the humour in the name, but did the owners understand they'd named their dining establishment after an invasive trash species related to the common goldfish?

They arrived at the restaurant at precisely seven p.m.

"I'm sorry, but your table's not quite ready yet," the hostess said. "May I show you to the lounge until we're able to seat you?"

Charlie shrugged. "Sure."

As they entered the space, Carrie pointed at the bar and whispered, "Oh, my God." It was a giant aquarium that ran the entire length of the room and reached from the floor to its clear glass top. As they took their seats, Charlie marvelled at the way the bar had been designed so that the fish swam in front of their legs and under the patrons' drinks.

"What can I get you this evening?" the bartender asked.

Charlie looked at Carrie. "White wine?"

"A bottle of chardonnay, please," she said to the man behind the tank. Charlie jumped as an octopus suction-cupped its way under his left hand.

By the time the octopus had moved on, the bartender had delivered their bottle and two wine glasses.

Carrie raised her drink. "To us and your new eight-legged friend."

They clinked glasses.

"I'm sorry Declan couldn't make it," Charlie said. "I was hoping that you'd have some time to get to know him a bit better."

Carrie smiled. "That man seems to really like his work."

"Yeah. You can say that again."

"Well, it's probably for the best that he isn't here because there's something I want to talk to you about," she said, sliding her hand onto his.

Charlie remembered the last time she'd said that, when she thought she was pregnant. His expression must have betrayed his thoughts.

"Don't worry," she said. "I'm not gonna have a baby."

The moment was interrupted by the hostess. "We're ready for you. If you'll follow me."

She led them to a small table stuffed in the corner of the dimly lit dining room. A stream of bubbles moved steadily up the clear glass walls and swirling lights danced on the ceiling giving the impression of dining underwater.

"I wonder if the little mermaid will be our server tonight?" Carrie asked.

A woman in a glittering top and sea-shell breastplates approached and introduced herself.

"My name is Ariel, and I'll be taking care of you this evening."

Charlie choked on his wine. Carrie pounded him on the back until he could breathe again.

Ariel handed them their menus. "I highly recommend the Salposar. It's the chef's specialty. He stuffs a salmon with a pollock that's stuffed with a Spanish sardine. Then it's served with a purée of fresh kelp. The fish will be deboned at your table by Frank, our master filletologist. It makes a perfect meal for two," she added.

"It's a marine turducken," Charlie whispered.

"We'll do it," Carrie said.

Once Ariel had departed, Charlie put his hand on Carrie's. "Okay. Tell me what's on your mind."

He moved his chair closer to her. Charlie could always tell when she was having man-problems. "So, who is he?"

A soft smile spread across her face.

"You pegged it," she said.

He quickly filled up her glass. "I know you better than anyone else. Tell me everything."

"Well...he's perfect. He's kind, considerate and really cute. And he's the greatest cuddler."

"And what's the problem you're having with this world champion cuddler?"

Carrie leaned in. "Well, for starters, I think he's afraid of commitment."

"Only an idiot wouldn't want to commit themselves to you," Charlie said.

"He seems to be far more concerned about how a relationship will affect his job."

"Well, what kind of guy puts his job ahead of someone he cares about?" he asked.

Carrie just stared at him.

The penny finally dropped. Charlie sat up straight. "Hey, unfair. You tricked me."

"No. I just opened the door and you walked right in."

"We're here to talk about *your* problems, not mine," Charlie said.

"But *you*, sweet man, are my problem. I'm concerned about you. You're piling up unresolved problems on top of unresolved problems and I don't think those shoulders of yours are built to hold that much weight."

Carrie refilled his glass then reached across the table. She grasped his hands and said, "Talk to me."

Charlie stared into his lap. "The stress is killing me!"

He pulled away from her grasp and started rubbing the heels of his hands into his thighs.

"I'm terrified about screwing up at work. I mean, what the fuck do I know about being a detective? And you can add that to everything else I don't know."

"Like what?"

"Like relationships. I've never had one before, at least not a romantic one. And to have the first one with a guy like him…it's like I chose climbing Everest as my first hike!"

"Trust me, Charlie. No one knows what the fuck they're doing when it comes to loving someone."

"I'm worried he'll get bored of me. I mean, he's exciting. I'm…Charlie."

"Well, as a friend, I can say that you are *not* boring, and I've known you for a lot longer than he has. You're a beautiful man, full of beautiful surprises."

Charlie continued, "And then there's my parents. Their brains pretty well exploded when they found out where I was working. Can you imagine what they'd do if they found out I'm in a relationship with Declan? I can just see it now. 'Oh, Mom and Dad, you know that guy you blamed for almost killing me? Well, we're dating now. Oh, and by the way, in case you haven't guessed, I'm gay! But don't worry, I fuck *him*, not the other way around, so that makes it okay.'"

Carrie burst out laughing. "Declan's a bottom? I never would have guessed."

"Well, he is with me, but that's not the point."

"So, what is the point?"

Charlie shook his head. "I'm having trouble figuring out if I can be with him and work with him at the same time."

Carrie took a deep breath. "Okay. So which is more important to you?"

"Both."

"That's not helpful," she replied. "You want my honest opinion?"

Charlie sat back in his chair. "Maybe. All right. Go ahead."

"I think you should keep your job. Has he ever said that he's unhappy with your work?"

"No. In fact, he offered to hire someone to take on the admin work so I could focus more on cases."

Carrie raised her glass. "Good! So that's settled then." She took a swig of wine.

Charlie drummed his fingers on the table. "But what about the relationship stuff?"

Carrie stared him directly in the eyes. "I'm not the one to answer that. You need to find a quiet time with Declan and tell him how you're feeling. And if he cares about you, you can work it out together. Do you think you can do that?"

Charlie looked down.

"Charlie. The problem isn't going to go away by itself. Text him. Text him right now and tell him you want to set up a time to talk."

"Okay, I'll do it." Charlie reached for his phone, then put it down. "I just can't do it now."

Carrie sighed. "Okay, maybe I'm pushing too hard. I know you'll do it when the time's right. You always know when to say the right thing. That's why I love you so much. That's why you're my best friend. And if things don't go the way you want, don't worry, there's plenty of fish in the sea."

As if on cue, Ariel and the man Charlie assumed was Frank arrived with their meal. Ariel set up a folding table which the man placed a covered silver platter on. She removed the cover with a dramatic flourish. "Your Salposar!"

Charlie stared at the three-headed monster on the platter. He wasn't prepared for a sardine head emerging from the mouth of the pollock which was peering out of the mouth of the salmon. It was straight out of a cartoon…or a horror film. Frank brandished his culinary weapons and in a flash had decapitated the meal, stripped it of its skin and bones, and offered up its flesh to them.

"Some of each?" he asked.

"Yes, please," Carrie squeaked out.

Once Frank had left with the remains of the seafood slaughter, Charlie looked down at his plate of neatly laid out fish resting on a bed of green mush, with a single potato artfully placed at the side. Charlie's stomach lurched. "This is…too much. Do you mind if we get the bill and head over to the Black Bean Eatery for something edible?"

Carrie nodded. "I thought you'd never ask."

Chapter Six

Declan was about to get out of his van, but changed his mind when he saw a woman heading toward Archie's place. She had come from the property next door and based on the light coat she was wearing, it didn't look like she expected to be outside for long. She pulled down all of the yellow police tape surrounding the scene, rolled it into a bundle then stuffed it into Archie's garbage can. She brushed off her hands, then headed back to her house and went inside.

She's got balls. She probably thinks that the police tape reflects poorly on her house. Maybe she's thinking of selling.

If there were any police watching, they certainly didn't seem concerned about the neighbour's actions.

Declan smiled.

Well, if it's not easily identifiable as a crime scene, no reason not to go in.

He drove halfway down the block and parked the van, then reached behind his seat and grabbed a box of printer paper he'd accidentally left in the back. Declan opened it, and removed a couple of packs of paper. He replaced them with a few items he pulled from the glove compartment, then carried the box back toward Archie's place. If anyone asked what he was doing, he'd tell them it was an evening delivery for Mr Whitcher.

Declan checked to see if any other neighbours were out, but there was no sign of anyone. He carefully made his way up the icy driveway then followed the walkway to the side door of the house. He tried the handle of the outer screen door with his gloved hand and was relieved to find that it was unlocked. Declan took another quick look around to make sure no one was watching, then tried his luck with the wooden inner door. The wood around the lock was slightly splintered as if the door had been forced open at one time.

When?

He turned the knob and gently applied his weight to the door and the lock eased its way out of its hole and dropped to the floor inside.

Someone else has already been here.

He took one last look around, pushed the door open and entered.

Declan set the box on the floor, took out a small flashlight and flicked it on. A quick look at the door lock from the inside told him that the damage wasn't recent. The door had been forced open a long time ago. Where the screws used to be, there were now just ragged holes. The lock had just been shoved back into place for show.

"You lazy bugger." Obviously, Archie hadn't been too concerned about his security. Maybe he should have been.

Declan removed a pair of disposable booties from the box. He slid them over his shoes, then walked up the half-flight of stairs into the main floor hallway. He pulled out his phone and photographed as he went.

The place smelled of cigarette smoke and greasy cooking. He poked his nose into the kitchen. There was a day's worth of dishes in the sink. Declan was surprised there wasn't more.

He walked down the hall. All the doors were open, except one. He started with what he thought might be Archie's bedroom. The bed was unmade and some clothes had been tossed onto a chair in the corner. On the single nightstand was an ashtray.

Bad move, Archie. You don't want to burn, do you? he thought as he remembered Freddy.

Behind the ashtray stood an old bedside lamp and beside it, a four-by-five framed picture of Freddy. Declan picked it up. It was different than the school photo of the boy that Declan had back in his office. Both photos showed Freddy from the waist up, but this was more informal. In this picture, Freddy was laughing and wore a brightly coloured T-shirt. He looked more alive.

Before placing the photo back on the nightstand, Declan took a picture of it.

How could your dad do what he did to you? And why did he keep a reminder of it so close?

Declan doubted if his own father had ever had a picture of *him* on his bedside table.

He left Archie's room and headed down the hall, past the bathroom, to the room with the closed door. Declan grabbed the doorknob, turned the handle and walked inside.

It was a bedroom, and plain, like the other rooms. The only difference between this room and the rest of the house was that this one was tidy. The bed was made and there was a small stuffed bear leaning up against the pillow. On the nightstand was a red toy car and a picture of a woman holding a baby. He picked up the picture and turned it over in his hand. He opened the frame to look at the back of the picture. In small neat print were the words

Marsha and Freddy – three days old.

He placed it back in the frame and put the photo back on the nightstand. The room was a shrine to a kid that Archie had supposedly hated. Something didn't fit.

A voice cut through the darkness. "And who the fuck are you?"

Declan spun to look back through the door to the hallway. The woman who had been ripping down the police tape stood in front of him. This time she was holding an old shotgun and it was pointed at his chest.

"Do you have to point that thing at me? Guns make me nervous," Declan said.

In truth, guns didn't make him nervous. Scared people with guns did.

"I'll be the one askin' the questions here," she said.

"Okay. And I'll be the one answering them."

"Let's start with who the hell are you and what the fuck are you doin' in Archie's house?"

"I'm Declan Hunt. I'm a private investigator. I used to be a cop. I was the guy who found the body of Archie's kid, Freddy."

The gun in the woman's hand started to waver. Given the lightness of her build, Declan figured that she was noticing the weight of the gun. He hoped that it didn't cause her to do anything stupid, like accidentally pull the trigger.

"You still haven't told me what you're doin' here."

She braced the gun against her shoulder and sighted down the barrel. If she'd never used a shotgun before, she was doing a damned good job of pretending she had.

Declan put his hands in the air. "I heard from the police today. They told me that Archie had been killed. But before he died, he passed on a message to the cops that was meant for me."

She pondered this for a moment. "Do the cops usually act as your messenger service?"

"Sometimes. Did you see a big cop here today? Three stripes on his coat sleeve?"

She nodded. "Grey-haired? Seems to like givin' orders? Yeah, he interviewed me. I think he said his name was Sawchuck."

"He was my partner when I was on the force. He's the one that gave me the message."

"That doesn't explain why you'd break into the scene of the crime," she persisted.

Declan smiled. "I wouldn't know it was a crime scene, would I? Someone tore down all the police tape."

She scowled. "It makes the neighbourhood look bad. They don't need the tape to investigate, do they? Now back to you. How do I know that you're who you say you are? For all I know you're the guy who killed Archie."

Declan took a deep breath. "I can prove who I am. Let me show you my PI licence."

She stared at him for a moment then flicked on the bedroom light. "Okay, but move slowly and I wanna see your hands at all times. And I'm not puttin' down the gun."

Declan kept both hands in the air as he slowly turned so that his back pants pocket was visible.

"I'm going to carefully take my wallet out now," he said.

He turned back to face her as he extracted his laminated ID card from the wallet and handed it to her. She had a good look at the licence.

"Now do you believe me?" Declan asked.

"Seems legit," she replied as she handed it back.

"Look," he said, "I'm just as curious about who killed Archie as you are. I just want to ask a few questions, then I promise I'll get out of here."

The woman lowered the gun. "Well, if we're gonna do this, we're not gonna do it here."

Declan nodded. "That's probably for the best, it being a crime scene and all."

"We'll go back to my house. And no funny business."

"I promise," Declan said. "There's just a few things I have to do so no one knows I've been here."

"Whatever. Do what you have to do, Columbo."

Declan turned off the bedroom light and closed the door. At the side entrance to the house, he took a few minutes to put the lock back in its rightful place from the inside, then picked up his box of supplies. As the two left by the front door, she pulled out a key from her pocket.

"Here. Hold this," she said handing Declan the gun. She pulled the door tight with one hand and locked the door behind her with the other.

She pointed to the gun. "I'll take that back now, if you don't mind. Not that it matters. It's not loaded anyway. It belonged to Archie, although he never liked guns. That one was his father's. He gave it to me in case any trouble came by while he was…away. I'm Katherine, by the way. Katherine O'Grady."

"Nice to meet you, Katherine O'Grady."

Declan followed her across the snow-covered lawn. He scanned the windows of the neighbours' houses to see if anyone was spying on them, but most had their curtains drawn against the cold January evening.

Katherine opened her door and invited Declan in. "Make sure you take off your booties," she said.

She led him into her kitchen and propped the gun in the corner. "I'll put that away later. You drink?" she asked.

"Yeah."

"Good."

She stepped out of the room and returned in a few moments with two small glasses and a bottle of emerald-green liquid.

"*Crème de menthe*?" she asked.

"That would be nice," Declan lied.

"Have a seat," she said as she sat down across from Declan and poured two drinks.

Declan took a sip and tried not to wince.

"Katherine, it looks like you knew Archie well."

"You could say that. I looked after his house when he was in jail, then looked after him when he got out."

"Was he in jail a lot?"

"Oh, you know. Whenever he needed some money, he'd go and do somethin' stupid and get caught."

"Do you know what sort of things he did?" he asked.

She stared at him.

Declan continued, "It might lead to a clue as to who killed him."

Katherine gave him a cockeyed look. "Mainly petty theft, but sometimes he'd let people store things at his place."

"Things?"

"Well, I'd sometimes see a truck back into his driveway and guys'd unload lots of boxes. I assume they stored 'em in his basement...and sometimes he'd have people stay at his house for a while. Look, I know what he was doin' probably wasn't legal. Archie really was an idiot, but he meant no real harm. He had his faults, as you've probably guessed from what happened to Freddy."

Declan pulled out his notepad. "Do you mind if I take some notes?"

"Go ahead. Where was I?"

"You were talking about Freddy," Declan said.

Katherine continued, "Archie wasn't what you'd call *open* to new ideas, like havin' a gay son. Yeah, I knew all about Freddy, and I knew it didn't sit well with his father that Freddy was gay. Archie *did* have a short fuse, but as he got older and his health started to fail him, he mellowed. He was a faithful old dog."

Are we talking about the same man?

"What about Freddy's mother? Marsha, was it?" Declan asked.

"She died when he was ten. Just dropped dead. It turned out she was born with a bad heart. Freddy was devastated. Archie, he wasn't built to raise a son on his own."

Declan's neck muscles tensed. "Not built to raise a son? From the police reports and the interviews they did with some of the people in the neighbourhood, it

49

was indicated that Archie had beaten the boy. There wasn't much left of him when they found Freddy, but what they did find showed signs of abuse."

Katherine leaned in toward Declan. "I don't remember the police ever interviewing me back then, but I can tell you this—Archie truly missed his son after he died. He really did. There wasn't a birthday that went by that he didn't acknowledge in some way. He swore that one of these days, he was gonna find out who killed him and make them pay."

Declan looked up from his notebook. "Freddy's death was ruled accidental, but you're saying Archie thought someone killed him?"

She snorted. "Anyone who knew anythin' about Freddy knew he wouldn't have been dumb enough to build a shelter out of wood and light a fire in it. The fact that the police wrote it off as accidental was an insult— not just to Freddy but to all of us. Just because he didn't come from money didn't mean he was stupid."

She smacked her empty glass down on the table. "I bet if Archie had money, he could've afforded to prove it was murder. I don't think the investigation went too deep." She paused then cocked her head. "Wait a minute—you said *you* found Freddy. Weren't you involved in the investigation?"

Declan stared her down. "I did find him, but it wasn't my case. And the cop in charge deep-sixed it. You're right—the rich get priority. The homeless, the poor, minorities—not so much. I want to make sure that doesn't happen here."

She nodded.

Declan continued. "So…do you know anyone who would want to kill Archie?"

She thought about it. "No one lately. Archie's been clean for a while now. Look, I know he was into a whole lotta stuff in the past, but that was then — before Freddy got burnt. The truth is, he was really busted up when young Freddy died. He gave up drinkin' like he kinda wanted to make up for the way he'd treated the boy."

Declan's thoughts swirled. *None of this makes sense. This isn't the Archie Whitcher I met.*

Declan needed to refocus his thoughts. "Did you notice anybody strange hanging around the house lately? Maybe even the day he was attacked?"

"I saw a stranger comin' down the street this mornin'. He stopped in front of my house and might've been lookin' toward Archie's place. I already told the police about him."

Declan nodded. "Had you ever seen him before? Was he one of the people who hid out at Archie's in the past?" he asked.

"No. Never. Those guys weren't that fancy."

"What do you mean by fancy?" Declan pushed.

"He had one of those expensive, long, light-brown coats. And a hat. He looked like a stylish gangster. Want a refill?" she asked, picking up the liqueur bottle.

"Thanks, but I'd better not. I'm driving."

She refilled her own glass.

"What was Freddy like?" Declan asked.

"He was a bit quiet unless he was havin' a fight with his dad. I remember the day Archie found out about Freddy's tattoo. He went ballistic. Archie told me he felt his son was no better than a prison butt-boy. That's a —"

"Yeah, I know what that means. Did you ever see the tattoo?"

"I never saw it, but Archie said it looked like it was done with a large safety pin and a ballpoint pen. He said it was a heart with the initials of Freddy and the boy he was seein'."

Interesting.

"What do you know about him — the other boy?"

"Not much. I saw them together once, down at the Tim Hortons. They were clustered together in the corner, gigglin' away about somethin'."

"You didn't happen to catch a name, did you? Could it have been Milo?"

"No idea. The other boy was a cute kid. Looked a bit older than Freddy, but at that age, you really can't tell, can you?"

"No, I guess you can't. One of the joys of puberty."

Katherine laughed.

"One thing I did notice about him," she continued, "he came from money."

"Oh?"

"Those clothes he was wearin' did not come cheap."

"I know it was a long time ago, but do you remember if you mentioned this other boy when the police were looking into Freddy's death?" Declan asked.

"I told you — the police didn't bother to interview me."

"Right. You did say that." Declan looked at his watch. "Well, Katherine, I really must be going. If you think of anything else, give me a call."

He gave her one of his cards and made his way out of the house.

As he walked back to his van, Declan could feel her eyes on him. He got into the vehicle, pulled out his cell phone and called his old partner again. The call went directly to voice mail.

"You've reached Gary Sawchuck. You know what to do." *Beeeep.*

"Gary. Declan here. Look, I've been thinking about Archie's murder case and that last thing he said to you—I'm wondering if it might have something to do with Freddy's death. Is there any way I could have a look at Freddy's file? And maybe Archie's past record. Give me a call back."

Chapter Seven

It was nine-thirty at night when Charlie mounted the stairs to the office. The lights were off. Charlie went up to the third-floor apartment but Declan wasn't there.

"Where are you?" Charlie said to himself. Maybe Declan had gone to Bar-None.

Charlie would give it 'til midnight before he'd call Mickey at the bar to find out if Declan was there.

His stomach grumbled. Dinner at the Black Bean had made up for the attempted meal at Carp Diem, but he still needed more food to soak up the wine. Charlie began rummaging through Declan's cupboards. All he found was protein powder, beans and some oatmeal. How could Declan survive with no snack food? Not even a bag of chips!

Charlie opened the fridge and found nothing more than eggs and milk. It would have to do. After all, desperate times called for desperate measures. He opened up the milk carton, put it to his lips and took a huge mouthful of curdled lumps of soured milk, then gagged and spewed it into the sink.

"Fuck fuck fuck fuck fuck!"

Charlie ran to the bathroom, flushed his mouth out with cold water, then rinsed with mouthwash. It became clear that if he wanted a snack, he'd have to go to the corner store and pick up some real food. He wiped his face dry with a towel.

A creaking sound came from the other room.

"Declan?"

There was another creak.

Charlie cautiously walked back into the main part of the apartment, but nobody was there.

"Jesus! Get a grip. It's just the building. Old buildings creak. I'm drunk and imagining things. I just need a little more food to help me sober up."

Charlie headed to the stairs, stopping to pick up one of Declan's dumbbells just in case someone was hiding down below. The first weight he reached for was too heavy to lift. After trying several, he settled on the smallest. It was light enough to manoeuvre, but heavy enough to knock someone out.

He crept down the stairs and into Declan's office, listening closely.

Nothing.

He looked at Declan's desk. It was clear of any clutter. Or it should have been. It *had* been when he went upstairs... Hadn't it?

Sitting on the desk, right under the beam from the track light, was the framed photograph of Freddy Whitcher.

That wasn't there before... Was it?

He walked around the desk and there was another creak.

Charlie looked around, then down. He was standing on a patched piece of flooring. He wiggled, and the floor creaked again.

"You are such a child."

Charlie reached for the photo, planning to put it back on the credenza where it normally sat. He wondered when the picture was taken. Freddy looked so formal. It must have been a school photo.

As Charlie looked up, he caught a reflection in the glass, like someone was passing behind him. He gasped and spun around, tightening his grip on the dumbbell.

There was nothing.

He had to get out of here. He was imagining things. Charlie turned to head back upstairs to return the dumbbell when he heard another creak coming from the stairs leading to the third floor. He dropped the dumbbell and high-tailed it out of the building.

He felt better being out in the frigid air even though he had left his coat behind.

Charlie turned to the right toward the nearby convenience store. He bought a bag of all-dressed potato chips, then went back out into the cold, munching on the snack as he headed back to Declan's. As Charlie approached the street-level door to the office, he walked straight into a man's chest. The chip bag was crushed and erupted all over both of them.

Charlie looked up. "I'm so sorry, I wasn't looking where I was going."

"Hey, Charlie," the other guy said.

He was tall and broad, but in the darkness between the street lights Charlie couldn't clearly make out his facial features.

"Do we know each other?" Charlie asked.

"We must, 'cause someone who didn't know me wouldn't have gone to the trouble to ruin my fuckin' life!"

The guy shoved Charlie backward and he fell to the ground. The man stepped toward him. He was now visible in the light. Charlie recognised him from his picture. It was Tyler Chipping.

"I heard from a couple of girls in my office you were asking a lot of questions about me. They said you were going to get me fired."

He kicked at the sole of Charlie's boot.

"You know, if you weren't such a publicity slut, getting your picture out there so often with that muscle-bound himbo of yours, I wouldn't have even known who you were."

Charlie crab-walked backwards.

Chipping stepped closer, weaving a little as he moved in. He was drunk.

Charlie bounced up onto his feet.

Tyler leered. "Jeez, you sure move well. I'd have thought you'd have been a little stiffer. Being that Hunt-guy's play toy must cause a lotta wear and tear on a little guy like you."

Chipping grabbed Charlie by the shoulders and slammed him against the brick wall next to the office door.

"Now let's see if Hunt'll wanna keep you once I've smashed in that pretty face of yours."

Tyler pulled back his fist. Charlie leaned in closer and quickly raised his knee, connecting with Chipping's unprotected groin, then leapt away from the man's crumpling body.

Tyler Chipping rolled on his side and groaned loudly before springing back to his feet. His fury was obviously overriding his pain.

"I'm gonna fuckin' kill you!" he screamed as he threw himself toward Charlie. Without thinking, Charlie rotated his body so that he was sideways to the oncoming attack. He threw all of his weight onto his back foot and rapidly extended his leg, arcing it toward Tyler, striking him hard on the side of his torso. Chipping collapsed onto his knees like a sack of potatoes.

Charlie leaned over him. "Now get the fuck away from my door. And I swear, if I ever hear you talking about Declan like that again, I will tear your limbs off and shove them down your fucking throat!"

Just then another figure appeared from the darkness of the alley beside the building. Charlie wasn't sure if he could handle a second attacker. He needn't have worried. It was Declan.

"Are you all right?" Declan called out to Charlie.

"Never fuckin' better!" Charlie replied. "Declan – this is Tyler Chipping. It seems like there's been some kind of misunderstanding. But he's leaving now. Isn't that right, Tyler?"

Tyler stood up. He was shaking. It was hard to tell if it was from rage or fear.

"My partner asked you a question," Declan said.

"Yeah, I'm leaving," he muttered, then limped off like a whipped dog.

Declan took Charlie by the shoulders. "Are you sure you're okay?"

Charlie smiled. "Absolutely."

"Where did you learn to roundhouse kick like that?"

"I guess from my karate training when I was a kid. It just all came back to me. So you saw that?"

"As a matter of fact, I did."

The adrenaline coursed through Charlie's body and one thought raced through his brain—*He didn't have to save me. I did it on my own.*

Declan put his arm around Charlie and led him through the door. "Come on, Bruce Lee. I think you deserve a stiff drink."

Declan sat Charlie down on the small couch in the apartment, then grabbed a bottle of scotch from the kitchen counter. He poured out a healthy shot for each of them.

"Here," Declan said. "Drink."

Charlie raised his glass, then with a weak grin, clicked his glass on Declan's. They both took hefty swigs.

"You were amazing out there, you know," Declan said.

Charlie nodded.

"You handled that guy like a pro."

He reached up and put his hand on Charlie's shoulder. "I know what you're feeling right now. You're coming down from an adrenaline high. You're probably in a bit of shock."

Charlie said nothing. He took another sip of scotch.

"Why don't I tell you what I've been up to? It'll take your mind off of your big adventure."

Charlie nodded. "Okay."

"I found out some surprising things about Archie Whitcher tonight," Declan started.

"Oh," Charlie replied.

"He seems to have found God, or something like that after Freddy died. He converted Freddy's bedroom into almost a shrine."

Charlie focused on his glass.

"I met his neighbour," Declan continued. "An interesting character. She took care of Archie. I'm just trying to figure out how deep their relationship went—"

"It's always going to be this way, isn't it?" Charlie interrupted.

"What way?"

"The job comes first...before us."

"Why would you say that?"

"You didn't even ask how dinner was."

Declan pulled back. Charlie shifted on the couch and faced him. "I really wanted tonight to be about us. I wanted you to spend some time with Carrie. I wanted you to get to know her, and her to get to know you a bit more. She's really important to me. More important than most of my family. She *is* my family, you know. And then I got home, and you weren't here. And then Tyler Chipping attacked me—"

"Look, I'm sorry about dinner tonight. I—"

"I just wish you'd let the police deal with this, but you couldn't put it off for one night, could you?"

Charlie stood up. "I'm feeling a bit sore. I'm going to go take a hot shower."

He stormed off into the washroom, peeled off his clothes and threw himself into the shower.

Charlie let the water flood over him. He wondered if he and Declan could ever have a *normal* relationship, whatever that was supposed to look like.

He closed his eyes and let the water begin to relax his muscles. After a few minutes, Declan stepped into the shower and pressed his body into Charlie's. Charlie felt Declan's coarse chest hair against his back.

Declan reached around and took the soap from the shelf. He lathered up his hands in front of Charlie, then slowly soaped up Charlie's chest, stomach and below.

Declan leaned his head into him. He kissed Charlie's ear and whispered, "I'm sorry. I'm not used to putting someone else first. I'll try to do better."

Charlie turned. "You promise?"

"I promise."

Declan paused. "Do you believe me?"

Charlie looked Declan in the eye. "I believe you'll try. And, for now, I guess that's gotta be good enough."

Chapter Eight

Declan woke to find Charlie snuggled into him. He smiled and buried his face in Charlie's curly blond hair, inhaling his scent. His reverie was interrupted by his phone which lit up with an incoming call.

Declan eased himself out from under Charlie, grabbed the phone from the bedside table and swiftly crept across the room. He answered the call, whispering "Just a sec," then muffled the phone against his chest and made his way down the stairs to the office. Once the door to the apartment was shut, he continued out to the reception area before saying, "Sorry about that."

"I don't even have to guess what's going on at your place," the voice of the caller said.

"Hi Gary. Thanks for getting back to me." Declan flopped his naked body onto the couch.

"I got your message. So, you want the Freddy and Archie Whitcher files." Gary said.

"I just have to know if there was anything that was missed in the initial investigation. What Archie said to you... My gut says it might lead to a clue we didn't know existed back then."

"Or it might mean nothing," Gary replied.

"That's true. But I'll never know unless I follow the lead," Declan said. "So, can you help me? Can you get me the files?"

"Only if you promise to minimise the chaos that you unleash."

"Deal."

Gary laughed. "Good. Meet me at eleven this morning in the restaurant at the Airliner Hotel. It's just south of the airport."

"I know the place. And Gary, thanks. I owe you big-time."

Declan disconnected, then stood up to return to the apartment. When he turned around, Charlie was standing there, naked.

"Sorry," Declan said. "I was just..."

Charlie shrugged. "It's fine. After all, it's a workday and we have no other plans. Do what you gotta do."

Declan noticed that Charlie had a morning erection. "Well, we don't open the office for another hour, so I think there's something I gotta do right now."

Charlie giggled as Declan chased him back upstairs to the apartment.

* * * *

Three hours later, Declan sat at a table by the window of the Airliner Hotel's restaurant. From where he was seated, Declan had a view of the mounted DHC-3 situated by the road. The decrepit 1950s bush plane clashed with the brutalist modern design of the hotel and the plane's wings were definitely in need of a good de-icing. It wasn't what Declan would have chosen to greet travellers as they made their way to and from the airport.

He'd arrived early, so had ordered a coffee. The waitress, Fran, swung by and also dropped off a piece of dry toast.

"You'll probably need this. Our coffee's like battery acid so your stomach'll appreciate it. Don't tell the manager I said so."

"Your secret's safe with me," he said with a big smile.

She headed off to the kitchen.

Declan looked over at the busboy. He was cute...probably younger than Charlie. Declan thought about what *he* had looked like in his twenties. Had people thought he was cute? He'd never considered it. Even back then. Everything he'd done, everything he had thought, was about fighting. Fighting with his father. Fighting with himself. Fighting with life. He'd been so filled with anger back then. Joining the police service was the last thing he should have done. Especially when he'd found out he was to be stationed in his father's district. He had thought there were rules against that, like in the army when brothers couldn't serve together. But obviously that was just in the movies.

Every muscle in Declan's body started to tense up. He remembered the exercises his therapist had taught him. He closed his eyes and took deep breaths. *In and out. In and out.* He visualised his muscles relaxing. First his toes, then his feet. All the way up his legs to the pelvis, and from his fingertips to his shoulders as he drifted into a trance.

"Excuse me. Would you like to order any food?" Fran interrupted.

He glanced at the clock on the wall. It was a quarter past eleven. He must have drifted off. *Where the hell is Gary?*

"I'm expecting someone. I'll give it five more minutes."

Just then, the door opened. Gary Sawchuck stomped the snow from his boots and made his way to Declan's table.

Gary looked just as he had more than a decade ago. He was tall, almost two metres in height, with silver-grey hair, dark-brown eyes and a clean-shaven square jaw. Declan had never mentioned it to anyone, but he'd developed a crush on him the first time he'd seen him.

Gary interrupted Declan's thoughts. "Christ. Three traffic accidents on the way here. It's like drivers have never been through winter before."

Gary pulled off his heavy winter coat and slipped it over the back of his chair. He dropped his still-fit frame into the seat across from Declan. Gary turned to the waitress. "Coffee, double cream and sugar, and a menu, please," he called out.

Fran brought Gary his coffee and a menu. He only glanced at it before ordering the all-day breakfast with bacon and eggs over easy and white toast with lots of butter.

Fran looked at Declan.

"Egg-white omelette, whole-grain toast, hold the butter please."

She wrote everything down and walked toward the kitchen.

"No wonder you still look in shape," Gary said. "It's good to see you again."

"Same here."

"So, from what I hear, you're making a bit of a name for yourself."

Declan rolled his eyes. "And sometimes it's a good name."

Gary laughed then drained half of his coffee in one long gulp. "Let's cut to the chase. So, what do you want to know?"

Declan leaned in. "Can you tell me what happened at Archie's place?"

"A 9-1-1 operator got a call from the house. The person on the other end just said 'police' and then stopped responding. They passed it on to us and we answered the call. By the time we arrived, Archie was in bad shape. There was blood all over the place."

Declan interjected, "And you were the first officer on the scene?"

Gary nodded. "As soon as we pulled up, I remembered the house. As strange as it seems, Archie recognised me."

"It's hard to forget a face like yours."

Gary ignored the comment. "He was having trouble breathing. He only lasted a minute after we got there. He passed along his message for you just before he died."

Declan signalled Fran for a coffee refill. Fran topped up both their mugs then headed back to the kitchen.

Declan asked, "And what exactly was Archie up to these days?"

"He was nothing but a low-end bookie and petty thief."

Declan looked at Gary. "Do you remember the day we told Archie his son was dead?"

"Yeah."

"Did that seem like a guy who cared about his kid?"

Gary pondered the question. "Not really. I'd say just the opposite."

"Exactly. It seems Archie did a one-eighty on his feelings toward Freddy."

Gary scowled. "And you know this how?"

"I *might* have gone to the house to take a look around after my dad gave me your message."

"Wait—you were in the house?" Gary asked.

"Yeah. And Archie had closed up Freddy's room and made it look like it was just waiting for him to come back."

"It's a crime scene, Declan. You don't just cross the yellow tape!"

"Thanks to a neighbour, there was no tape around the place when I got there."

"Jesus Christ!"

"Don't worry," Declan continued. "I was booted and gloved up. I didn't compromise the scene. Although the neighbour who tore down the tape saw me and visited me in the house. She had a key and apparently comes and goes, so signs of her were probably already there."

Gary put his face in his hands. "Who was this?"

"Her name's Katherine O'Grady," Declan replied.

"Wait a minute. We interviewed her. What did she say?"

"Did she tell you about the man in the coat?" Declan asked.

"Yes."

"She didn't offer much more than that…other than a glass of *crème de menthe*."

Sawchuck sighed. "I thought the day you left the force my life would get easier, but you still find ways to complicate things."

Declan pushed on. "The message Archie gave you — when the police interviewed the neighbours, did they talk to anyone named Milo?"

"Not a one."

"And the case notes from Freddy, was there any mention of a Milo in them?"

"The file's pretty thin. It was ruled an accidental death so there isn't much there."

Declan stared at Sawchuck. "Can I take a look?"

The waitress came back and set plates of food on the table. "Anything else, gentlemen?"

They both shook their heads and after she departed, the men ate in silence. After a minute Gary reached into a bag he'd been carrying and tossed a couple of files onto the table. Declan looked at the covers. The thinner of the two was the report on Freddy Whitcher. The larger was Archie Whitcher's past.

"You can't keep them," Gary said, "but no one's going to stop you from copying them. I don't have to tell you that if anyone finds out I've shared this with you, the only one who'll be in more shit than me will be you 'cause I'll be standing on your shoulders."

Declan picked up the file and called out to Fran, "Does the hotel have a business centre?"

Gary sighed loudly. "You do have a cell phone with a camera, don't you?"

Charlie would have thought of that right away.

Declan grabbed for his phone and started shooting.

Sawchuck frowned. "You know, you're a magnet for stuff like this, whatever *this* is. And whatever it is, I have a feeling it won't be nice."

His gaze burnt into Declan's skull. "And don't forget, what rains down on you is also going to soak anyone near you. So keep that in mind."

* * * *

Gary walked out of the restaurant with the files safely back in his possession. Declan signalled for a coffee refill and began poring over the images he'd taken of Freddy Whitcher's file, then read over the preliminary police report on Archie.

Declan made a list of questions.

Why did Archie want to send a message to me?
Who is Milo?
Who was the man in the coat on the street? Was he Milo? Did he kill Archie?
Who else would want Archie dead?
Does any of this have anything to do with Freddy's death?

Chapter Nine

Charlie opened his eyes. He stared at the ceiling for a minute before his hand reached out to Declan's side of the bed. Nothing. Declan was gone.

What time is it?

The clock on Declan's nightstand read 11:58 a.m.

"What the fuck?"

He'd slept the whole morning away. Not surprising given what they'd gotten up to after Declan's call from his old partner. *He should get calls like that more often.*

Charlie climbed out of bed, went to the bathroom and rinsed his mouth out with mouthwash. His head was muddy from sleeping too long. He made the bed, then a cup of coffee. As he padded around the apartment, Charlie remembered that they were supposed to be running a business and he should open up. He threw on a pair of khakis and a shirt and made his way downstairs where he was confronted by the mess that camouflaged his desk. Charlie sighed.

"Ad for my replacement first, then I'll tidy you up."

He carefully stacked all of the files and invoices on the floor to give him and his coffee cup a chance to work.

Charlie located a copy of his original job description on his computer. Other than sleeping with the boss, the job of office manager hadn't changed much since he'd started last year. He uploaded it to the same online job website that he'd used to get the job in the first place. His heart pounded as he hit 'Post'.

Charlie's train of thought was derailed by his stomach making a loud growl that sounded like a large cat trying to speak Swedish.

"Okay. Okay. Take it easy."

He pushed back his chair then made his way down to Gwen's café, *Les Trois Magots*.

"Good morning," he chirped as he entered.

Gwen shot him a glance. "I don't want to know why you're so chipper."

Charlie smiled. "Because it is a delightful, sunshiny winter's day!"

"The only thing you're missing are Snow White's birds flitting about," she said, wiggling her fingers around his head.

"Actually, what I'm missing is—" The cat in his stomach chattered away again.

"Ah, I see," Gwen said. "Will it be the usual? Or can I entice you with one of my new treats, a breakfast bun consisting of a savoury scone surrounding a fried egg and brie? Or Roquefort if you're more of the adventurous sort."

He smiled and said, "Sort of a high-end McMuff—"

"If you dare finish that sentence, you will be barred from this shop for at least a year."

From the look in her eye, Charlie knew she was serious.

"I think it sounds great. I'll take one with brie, and a chocolate croissant. Please."

A bag of baking in hand, Charlie mounted the stairs up to the office where he spent the next hour sorting all of the paperwork that had consumed his desk. He looked triumphantly at the now organised chaos that was stacked on chairs, the couch and the coffee table in the reception area. Filing would be next.

Charlie made his way to the kitchenette to clean up his coffee mug, and had just finished drying it when he heard the chirp that signalled the ground floor door opening. A second chirp announced the opening of the office door.

Charlie stepped back into the main room and saw a woman looking at his piles of paper. She appeared to be in her early seventies. "Can I help you?" he said.

"Possibly. Is Declan in?"

"No. He stepped out."

She looked at Charlie over the top of her glasses. "Do you expect him back any time soon?"

Charlie considered the question. "I'm not sure. He's in the field at the moment."

She nodded, but didn't move.

"Perhaps I can help you. I'm his assistant, Charlie Watts," he said, shaking her hand.

"Certainly not the drummer," she said. "You are far cuter, and have a much firmer handshake."

"Oh. So you've met Charlie Watts, from The Stones?" He had trouble concealing the scepticism in his tone.

"I certainly did," she replied. "It was October 2005 at the Saddledome. I gave him the ride of his life later that night. Nice fellow, though. Still sent me a card on my birthday 'til he died."

Charlie had been so engrossed in the woman's conversation that he hadn't noticed that the office door had opened and Declan had come in.

Declan was slapping his thighs from the cold. "Okay. I don't care what they look like, I think it's time I get a pair of long johns." He stopped in his tracks. "Oh—my—God! Mrs B!" Declan yelled, then ran over to the woman, lifting her off the ground.

"Mrs Beckerman?" Charlie said.

"What are you doing here?" Declan asked. "I thought you were down south, tanning yourself on a beach somewhere with your new boyfriend."

"I was 'til I realised how boring perpetual summer is. And as for Manuel…Well, he just wanted one thing, and it wasn't fun. I just had to get back up here where life was normal."

Charlie couldn't believe it. He never thought he would meet the legendary Mrs B, the woman whose job he had taken six months ago.

"Charlie—?" Declan started to ask.

"Oh, sorry. Mrs Beckerman, can I get you something?"

"Just a small coffee, black. One sugar. And I'd love one of Gwen's pastries if it isn't too much trouble."

Charlie nodded and headed down to the café on the ground floor.

* * * *

Declan ushered Mrs B to the couch. He moved several piles of paper off of it and placed them back on the desk. "Make yourself comfortable. I'll grab some plates and napkins from the kitchenette."

When he returned, she was flipping through the magazines on the coffee table. "These are the same magazines that were here when I left. I'm going to have to let Mr Watts know that they don't just replace themselves."

"Don't be too hard on him. He's trying his best."

"And I'm sure having to deal with you is a full-time job unto itself," she said.

"You'd know, wouldn't you."

Mrs B smiled and nodded. She raised a single eyebrow. "Last time you emailed me, you said he was cute, but I don't think you did him justice. And from the look in your eye, there's something more going on here than him just answering phones."

"As a matter of fact, that's true. Charlie's getting his PI licence and I've been shifting him into case work."

"That's *not* what I was referring to."

The door burst open and Charlie came in with a cardboard tray with three coffee cups and a bag held between his teeth.

"Gen fend ese uff. He fed —" Declan took the bag out of his mouth. "Gwen sent these up. She said they were your favourites. She's so excited that you're back in town."

"You see, I never got *this* down in Bogotá."

Charlie put the pastries and cookies down on the coffee table, then sat on a chair beside Declan, across from Mrs B.

She took a sip of her coffee. "So, Charlie. How's it been working for Declan? I hope you're not letting him off too easy."

Charlie looked at Declan. "It's definitely a challenging job. I understand you didn't let him get away with anything."

"Oh, he wasn't all that bad. Other than occasionally coming back bruised, bleeding and covered in garbage."

Charlie nodded. "Some things never change."

"So..." Mrs B smiled. "Declan says that you're moving into case work."

Charlie grinned. "I hope to have my PI licence in a couple of months."

"My God, you're even younger than he was when he started out," she said, pointing to Declan.

Declan didn't like the direction the conversation had taken. "So how long are you back for?" he asked, hoping to change the topic.

"For good, I suspect. I've moved in with my sister Irene until I can find a place of my own."

"And what will you do to pass the time?" Declan asked.

"I haven't given it any thought. My stay in Colombia after my heart attack taught me not to plan too far ahead. Opportunities can pop up at the last minute."

Declan smiled. "Funny you should say that. I know of an opportunity that might interest you. How would you feel about coming back here as our office manager? Charlie here can't handle the admin job on top of his case work."

She looked at the piles of paper stacked around the office. "So it would appear. But there's already two of you here. Where would I be working...if I said yes, that is?"

"Declan thought I could set up over there," Charlie said, pointing to the corner between Declan's office door and the window. "Eventually we could put up a wall so you wouldn't have me staring at you all the time. It would give you more privacy."

"That sounds sensible," she replied.

Declan turned to Mrs B. "What do you say? Do you want to rejoin Declan Hunt Investigations?"

She smiled. "I have a hunch that the two of you are going to need as much help as you can get. I was just popping in for a visit, but it might be fun to come back…for old times' sake."

"Is that a yes?" Declan asked.

"Yes," Mrs B said as she finished her coffee. "Well, I shouldn't take up more of your time. I'm sure you're very busy."

She stood.

"I'll start on Monday, if that's all right. By then maybe Charlie will have sorted out the desk situation." She turned to him. "You might want to check with Gwen. I believe she has a store of old office furniture left over from the previous tenants. I'm sure she'd be happy to see it put to good use."

She nodded curtly and headed to the door, then turned and said, "And thank you for not making me *ask* to come back. I've missed the old place."

Declan grinned. "While Charlie's sorting out furniture, do you have time for a bite to eat? Maybe a late lunch and a drink to celebrate?"

"Are you buying?"

"Of course."

"Then let's go."

Charlie said, "While you're having lunch, I'll pull the job posting I put up this morning."

Declan said, "Fantastic."

As they turned to go, Charlie asked, "You will take me seriously, won't you, Mrs B?"

She laughed. "I never took Declan seriously. Why should I treat you any differently? Now I expect these piles of paper to be filed before I come in on Monday."

She held out her arm to Declan and they made their way down the stairs and out of the building.

Chapter Ten

Charlie wandered into Declan's office and relaxed back into his chair, imagining what it would be like to have his very own space. He had just put his feet up on the desk when the door alarm chirped. Charlie quickly stood and stepped out into the main room. The door opened and a distinguished older man entered. He was in his late sixties, and dressed in a yellow puffy parka. He was about Charlie's height, was very well groomed and had misty grey eyes a shade darker than his hair. His appearance gave him an air of authority.

"May I help you?" Charlie asked.

"Some oxygen, if you've got it. Those stairs just about did me in."

"Please," Charlie said, "have a seat." He gestured toward the couch, then realised that the coffee table and floor still had piles of paper on them. "Sorry, we're just in the middle of reorganising the files. Perhaps you would be more comfortable in the office."

"That would be fine."

Charlie led the man into Declan's office, taking a seat behind the desk.

The man unzipped his coat and put it over the back of the other chair.

"Now," the man said as he sat down, "I have to apologise for not making an appointment, but I was in town for a doctor's visit and I thought, 'What the hell, give it a shot and see if anyone's at home.'"

"I'm sorry," Charlie said, "but if you're here to see Declan Hunt, he's not in at the moment."

The man's eyes widened. "Oh. How foolish of me. I am so sorry. I should have realised that you're not, I mean you don't look..."

"Rugged enough?" Charlie offered.

The man rose and reached for his coat.

"Wait. Maybe I can help. I'm Mr Hunt's assistant, Charlie Watts." Charlie extended his hand. The gentleman shook it.

Charlie continued, "Is it safe to assume that you're in the market for a private investigator?"

The man nodded. "I am indeed."

"Well, I often handle intake interviews for the firm," Charlie said. "If you feel comfortable enough, and since you're here, you can tell me about your concerns and I can produce a summary report for Declan. I'll see that he gets it when he returns."

The man settled back into his chair.

"Yes. Foolish of me not to make an appointment. I just thought... Well, Mr Hunt came highly recommended, so I don't imagine he would have hired a fool as an assistant. Where shall I begin?"

"Let's start with your name, address and a contact number. I'll fill out a preliminary non-disclosure agreement. That way, you can be assured that whatever you say is confidential from this meeting onward, whether we take your case or not."

The man smiled. "I like the way you work. All right, let's do this. My name is Simon Griffin. I live at — oh here..." He pulled out his wallet and produced a business card. "My address in Banff, and my home and cell numbers are all there for you."

Charlie had never met anyone who actually lived in Banff.

He must have money.

Charlie wrote out the pertinent information on the non-disclosure agreement, signed it then had Mr Griffin sign. After making a copy, Charlie pulled out his notepad and began, "Now, Mr Griffin, how can I help you?"

"I want you to find my son, Milo."

Charlie frowned. *Wasn't Milo the name Archie Whitcher said just before he died?*

Simon must have noticed the change in his expression. "Is everything all right?"

Charlie nodded. "Yes. So when is the last time you saw your son?"

"It would have been about ten years ago, just shortly after my birthday, which is January the third."

"Ten years ago? And you're only looking for him now?" Charlie asked.

It was Simon's turn to frown. "When Milo disappeared, I contacted the police. There was a full investigation by the RCMP, but it amounted to nothing. Then my assistant Tom conducted his own search with every resource I could provide. I even offered a reward, but it seemed Milo had simply disappeared. The police decided he was just another teen runaway. But I think he's come back."

Charlie looked up from his notes. "And why do you think that?"

"Because of this."

Simon produced a piece of paper which he placed on the desk.

I'm watching you and I know what you did.
Milo

Charlie let out a low whistle. "And when did you receive this note?"

"It was at the house a few days ago."

"I'm sorry to ask this, but why did you wait so long?"

Simon paused. "I was pondering if I should take it to the police, but decided I needed someone who could handle this with a bit more discretion. I don't want my name in the papers."

Charlie nodded. "And do you have any idea what this means? 'I know what you did.'"

Simon shook his head and looked down at his hands. "I have no idea. You have to understand that Milo was a teenager when he disappeared. And we didn't always see eye to eye on things. In fact, the last time I saw him, we'd had quite a bad argument, which is why the authorities initially thought he'd run away."

"What was the argument about?" Charlie asked.

"I have a vault in my office at home where I keep things of great value. Milo knew he wasn't supposed to go in there without my permission, but he had, and possibly had even removed something from inside. When I confronted him, he denied it. I was very angry and told him that if he didn't behave, I might have to kick him out and he would be forced to live with his mother. He said he had a much better idea. He was thinking that maybe it was time for him to move out on his own."

"How old was he at the time?" Charlie asked.

"Fifteen! I didn't think he was serious."

"And after he disappeared," Charlie continued, "did you try and get in touch with his mother?"

"Of course I did, but that was another dead end. She hardly knew him at all. She left him with me when he was a baby and never came back. You see, Michelle was an actress and always put her career first." The colour rose in Simon's face and he gripped the arms of the chair, his knuckles turning white.

"When I contacted her, she claimed she hadn't seen Milo. Still, I wondered if he might have thought going to her place would give him a more glamorous life with that B-grade film producer husband of hers. No, wait— that was the previous one. This one was a writer. That's it, a writer. And not even a literary one. This one churned out pop-lit trash at the rate a normal person would throw out their garbage, which was pretty much the same thing."

This wasn't going the way Charlie had hoped. *What would Declan do?*

"Would you like a glass of water?" He glanced around the room and saw the bottle of scotch on the credenza. "Or perhaps something stronger?"

Simon loosened the grip on his chair. "Perhaps something stronger would help."

"How about a scotch?"

Simon nodded his approval.

Charlie poured a healthy two fingers into a crystal glass and handed it to Simon

"Thank you," he said, taking the glass from Charlie and taking a sip. He smacked his lips. "Twelve-year-old Laphroaig, if I'm right."

Charlie nodded. "It was a birthday gift from our accountant."

"And to think, mine only sends me a card. I'll have to get your man's name."

The drink seemed to do the trick.

"So we were talking about your ex-wife," Charlie prompted.

Simon took a deep breath. "Yes. In spite of what she said, I had her under surveillance for a month just to be sure, but no sign of Milo."

"What is Milo's mother's full name?" Charlie asked.

"Michelle Coleman. She worked mostly in film in the States. I don't think she's working much anymore. As beauty fades, so does the career."

"Do you have an address or phone number for her?"

"Yes. I can get you that once I get home."

Charlie reviewed his notes. "And is there anyone else he was close to back then? Anyone I could try and track down?"

Simon sat up straighter in his chair. "There was a boy he was seeing. He was a bit younger than Milo and I'm pretty sure they were more than friends. As I've told you, it was a long time ago, so I don't remember much about him, but I recall he looked like he was from the wrong side of the tracks. Milo was careful not to bring him around the house but I saw them exchanging a kiss outside of a coffee shop in Banff one day. When I asked Milo about it, he said I must have seen somebody else."

"Did you know the boy's name?"

"No."

"Did you make any attempt to find the other boy?"

"The police looked into it, but said it was another dead end."

Simon paused as he looked at the picture of Freddy Whitcher on Declan's desk.

"Is that Mr Hunt's son?"

Charlie shook his head. "No. He doesn't have any children. Now, I have one more question for you, Mr Griffin."

Simon's gaze returned to Charlie.

"Did your son have access to money? A bank account, credit card, that sort of thing?"

"I insisted that he have a bank account. Young people have to know how to take care of their money. I had him on an allowance that I deposited in the bank for him every month."

"And was any money withdrawn before or after his disappearance?"

Mr Griffin sat in silence before answering. "After he vanished, I had a look at his bank statement. He'd been withdrawing five hundred dollars a month for the ten months before he disappeared."

"And nothing since?"

"I left the account open for a while, hoping it would show some activity, but it never did. I closed it long ago."

Charlie said, "Five thousand dollars is a lot for a kid to carry around."

Simon shifted in his chair. "That's not all. A few weeks after Milo disappeared, five thousand dollars was missing from petty cash reserves that I keep in the vault. I suspect it was Milo. So he actually had ten thousand dollars in cash at hand."

"And no one else had access to the vault?"

"Only my assistant, Tom. And before you suggest it could have been him, I assure you, to him, that amount means nothing."

Charlie looked over his notes. There was a lot to consider. "I think I have everything I need to get started, Mr Griffin. But before I do, is there anything else you'd like to add?"

"I'd like to get to the bottom of this, and if Milo is still around, I'd definitely like to see him."

Charlie nodded. "I'll go through this with Declan the moment he gets in and get back to you tomorrow. By the way, may I make a copy of this note for the file?"

"Not a problem."

Charlie stood. Mr Griffin eased himself out of the chair, sat down his empty glass on the desk, and followed Charlie out of the office. Charlie scanned the note, handed the original back to Mr Griffin, then walked him to the door.

"Thank you so much for coming in today, Mr Griffin. As I said, I'll give you a call tomorrow."

He shook Mr Griffin's hand.

"Thank you, too, Mr Watts. I look forward to hearing from you. And if I'm not in, just leave a message with my housekeeper, Jasmine. She'll make sure I get it."

* * * *

Simon returned to his 2001 navy-blue Bentley Arnage. It was the one possession he valued above all others. The Paddock could burn to the ground and he could move on, but anyone who put so much as a scratch on his car would feel his wrath.

Simon had left the car in a parking lot two blocks away. He had warned the twenty-something-year-old parking lot attendant to watch over it and given him fifty dollars. If he came back and the car had been properly taken care of, there would be another fifty in it for him.

When he arrived back at the lot, the young man was standing guard over the car. "No one touched it, sir."

"Good man," Simon said, patting him on the shoulder. He handed him the other fifty, and a twenty on top of it for doing such a good job.

Simon sat in the driver's seat and thought about the interaction he'd had with the young Mr Watts. Although Simon hadn't lied, he'd been particular about the facts he had revealed. But that wasn't what made him uneasy. It was that photograph—the one of the young boy. What was it doing in that room?

Chapter Eleven

Charlie quickly typed up the notes from his meeting with Simon Griffin. He sent the report to the printer, then put it on Declan's desk. When he came back into the main room, he looked around at the stacks of files and reports that still needed to be put away. Mrs B wouldn't be happy if she was greeted by this mess when she came in on Monday.

"No time like the present."

He filed what he could and put the rest back into a single pile on the coffee table. Then he went to the computer and deleted the posting for the job Mrs B had taken back. When he looked at the clock, it was two-thirty. His stomach announced in no uncertain terms that he had skipped lunch.

"Okay, okay. I'll feed you."

He locked the door and headed down to Gwen's.

As he entered, she asked, "Back again? So, what can I get my favourite customer this time?" The aromas of coffee and pastries that filled the air never failed to entice him every time he walked through the door.

"The usual, please," Charlie said.

"And what would that be? I mean, you seem to like everything I make—which I am thrilled with. How is it that you haven't gained an ounce since you started here?"

Charlie scanned the contents of her display case. She was right—he could easily order one of everything.

"I'll have a ham and brie croissant and a latte please. Oh, and for here."

She started to perform her magic behind the counter. Charlie leaned on the other side, watching her work.

"I have some great news for you," he started, but before he could finish, she interrupted.

"I know—Mrs B is coming back to work with you. Declan already told me when the two of them were heading out for lunch. Here," she said, sliding his plated sandwich toward him. "Grab a seat and I'll bring you your coffee."

He'd eaten most of the sandwich by the time she returned.

"So," Gwen began, "if Joan's coming back to the office, where will you be working?"

"Declan wants me to set up my own office space. Well, it won't be an office yet—more of a corner outside his, but he said we can get someone to throw up some walls and a door when we get some more money coming in."

He realised that he probably shouldn't be discussing the company's finances with her. "Forget I said that last part."

"It's forgotten."

"Good. Now, Mrs B said I should ask you about old office furniture that you might have stored away in the basement. Do you really have some down there that we could…borrow?"

She smiled. "No, but I've got some that you can have. Wanna go have a look?" She walked toward the back of the shop.

"Is it okay just to leave the café unattended?" he asked.

"It's late enough. No one other than you or Sam would be coming around. Just lock the front door and flip the 'Closed' sign around. Now, let me show you what I have in the basement."

As they walked toward the cellar steps, Gwen asked, "What do you need?"

"It's really just a corner of the main office space, so…a desk and chair. Maybe a filing cabinet and a bookcase."

Gwen flicked on the basement light switch then headed down. "Let's see what we can do for you. So…getting your own space. I'm proud of how far you've come in the last six months. Anyone that can put up with Declan for that long without walking out has accomplished a lot."

Charlie turned the corner into what appeared to be a furniture storage room. There were stacks of drawers and several disassembled desks piled on top of each other. A row of dark wooden bookcases lined one wall and a corral of chairs and filing cabinets filled the rest of the room.

"It's all been here since I set up shop and it's just taking up space. I've always meant to have a huge garage sale, but I never got around to it. Might as well start with you. What'll you have?"

Charlie started at one end and worked his way to the other. He pulled together the pieces of a beautiful old oak desk which had a single bank of drawers. He located a matching chair.

"What about this to go with it?" Gwen said, patting the top of a five-tier oak barrister's bookcase. "The glass on the doors is still intact."

"It's gorgeous," he said, running his hands over the dusty surface. "I think it would look perfect up there."

Charlie plopped down in the leather-upholstered wooden chair he'd chosen, spinning it around. It would do perfectly until he got something more ergonomic. Or maybe he would just keep this one. It felt...right.

Gwen stood in the dim light, smiling. "It all looks very Sam Spade. All you need is the trench coat and the fedora."

"Any idea whose furniture it was?" Charlie asked, patting the chair.

She smiled mischievously. "Well, the guys who owned the building before me were morticians. I assume it was theirs."

The word 'morticians' echoed in Charlie's ears.

Gwen continued, "Didn't you notice the sign carved into the stone above the door leading up to Declan's office? 'Hallowell Brothers, Undertakers'?"

Charlie shook his head.

"Well, it's just 'Hallowell Brothers, Under' right now," Gwen continued. "The rest is hidden under my sign. What's now the café was once their funeral chapel. They had their casket showroom upstairs, and their office was where Declan has his. The third floor was where they stored the extra coffins and I think they prepped the bodies down here in the basement. In fact, they used to have a retort over there where they cremated the bodies. The exhaust flue came in handy when I moved in and put in the bakery."

Charlie shuddered.

Gwen continued. "If you look at the floor in Declan's office, you'll see a patch of newer flooring. The same up in his apartment. They used to have a dumbwaiter for caskets so they wouldn't have to carry them down the stairs."

Charlie stared at her. "My beautiful new office space was once covered in coffins?"

Gwen shrugged. "I suspect this building probably has a few ghosts lingering around, but I've never seen any. Have you?"

Charlie paused. "Uh...nope."

Charlie could tell she didn't believe him.

"Oh, come on now," she said, breaking into a laugh. "You, of all people can't believe in that, can you?"

"Maybe just a little."

Gwen grinned. "You, my friend, are going to have to cut down on your caffeine and sugar intake immediately. Now, let's get this up to your office. The two of us can manage the lighter stuff. We'll have to wait for Declan to come home before we can tackle the heavier things."

"Hello?" a voice called from upstairs.

Charlie jumped.

"Down here in the cellar," Gwen yelled.

Charlie heard heavy footsteps and a familiar voice. "Your front door was locked so I came in the back. What are you doing down here?"

The large frame of Sam Hunt appeared around the corner.

"Perfect timing. You can give us a hand taking some of these pieces up to Charlie's new space. Things are getting serious up there. He's getting his own office."

Gwen smiled. "I've got some freshly baked scones that will make it worth your while if you help us."

Sam grinned. "I'd get my way more often if you weren't such a damned good baker."

It took a few hours, but Charlie and the others managed to get everything upstairs. The three of them were sweating from the exertion by the time everything was put together and in place, but it looked great. Charlie couldn't wipe the smile off his face.

"Don't offices usually come with walls?" Sam said from where he was lying on the couch.

Charlie piped up. "There's a plan to put up walls, but not just yet."

"The space is still missing something," Gwen said. "Some artwork. Something to suit the vibe of the old furniture."

"Like what?" Charlie asked.

"How about we find a photo of what this building used to look like when it was a funeral home —"

"A what?" Sam asked.

"Sam — don't interrupt." She turned back to Charlie. "We'll find an old picture and get it blown up. We could hang it above the bookcase," she said with a devilish smile on her face.

"Over my dead body," Charlie replied.

Gwen bent down and gave Charlie a kiss on the head. "Hopefully it never comes to that. Now, come on, Sam. Let's get those scones, then we can go home, get cleaned up and I'll take you out for dinner."

Sam shrugged his shoulders and they headed down the stairs, leaving Charlie alone.

He spent the next hour cleaning his desk and bookcase, then polished the leather chair with a soft cloth until it shone like new.

Charlie stood back and marvelled at his *bureau sans murs*, as the French would say — an office without walls. Gwen wasn't the only one around here with a deft hand at French and, like Gwen's *Les Trois Magots*, he'd be open to anyone in need. And, speaking of Gwen, there wasn't a hope in hell that he was putting up a photo of a mortuary above that beautiful bookcase. He'd hang his very serious-looking university diploma there. His credibility needed all the help it could get.

Just then, his eye caught a flash of something reflected in one of the bookcase glass doors. Charlie spun around. His heart raced. There was nothing. It must have been a reflection from the street below.

"You absolute wuss," he said, plunking himself down in his chair. This felt like it was the start to a new life. He slowly turned the chair on its pivot and out of the corner of his eye, inside the door to Declan's office, he swore he saw the shadow of a person. They were only there for a moment, then they were gone. This time it was no trick of the light. He was sure of it.

He sat motionless, staring at where the apparition had been. *Get a grip!* His heart was pounding out of his chest.

You are a rational human being. It's just an old building playing tricks on you... An old building that you are the only living person in.

Air moved past his cheek. He gasped. Then he swore a soft voice whispered, "Help me."

"Don't be stupid," he said to himself. "There's no such thing as ghosts."

When the stairs that led up to the apartment squeaked, it was too much.

Charlie grabbed everything he needed and ran down to his car. As he waited for it to warm up, he texted Declan.

Heading out early. Don't forget it's the annual Carrie/Charlie get-outta-town weekend. See you on Monday!

By the way, I had a visit from a promising client. Appears to be wealthy! His name's Simon Griffin. He's looking for his missing son, Milo. Coincidence? Report is on your desk for when you get back.

Smooches,

Me.

Chapter Twelve

Charlie hadn't slept well over the weekend. His slumber had been disrupted with dream after dream of people rising from the dead and walking around the office. He clearly remembered one ghoul in the kitchenette—a short young man wearing an old-fashioned black suit. His hands and feet were charred, and his face was a blotchy mess of blue and purple. He was missing an ear, as well as the left half of his face. He wore a name tag—Dave. In the dream, Dave had been trying to work the espresso machine. He had turned to Charlie and asked if he'd prefer a latte or a cortado. Charlie had woken up in a cold sweat. He wasn't getting back to sleep, so he got up, closed the door on Carrie's room then tip-toed to the bathroom. He showered and dressed, making sure that he didn't wake her up.

This morning, ghosts were not the only thing on his mind. Today was the first day back for the legendary Mrs B and he wanted her to like him.

He headed into work, making a pit stop at Declan's favourite health food shop, Chia Country—formerly Wheat Germ World, and before that, Pulse Planet. Charlie found none of the names compelling. In general, he disliked health food, but it was open twenty-four hours for anyone who needed a beet juice and celeriac smoothie—bee pollen extra—early in the morning. He bought a large Styrofoam cup of the vile concoction Declan liked to drink, then continued on his way to work.

Charlie parked the car in the lot behind the building and made his way to the front entrance of Gwen's café. He looked up. There, just to the left of her sign, carved into the sandstone lintel, were the words 'Hallowell Brothers, Under'.

How could I not have seen that before?

He stepped into Gwen's café.

"Morning, Charlie. You're here early," Gwen said.

Charlie stared bleary-eyed into the display case. He was having trouble focusing.

"You all right?" she asked.

"I'm sorry. Didn't get much sleep last night."

"Oh dear," she said. "I have just the thing for you."

Gwen plucked a couple of custard-filled Portuguese tarts from the display case and popped them gently into a bag.

"There," she said, smiling. "There's plenty of protein in the custard. You can pretend they're good for you."

Charlie also bought an americano for Declan and a double latte for himself then made his way up to the office, carefully balancing his load. He'd stuffed Declan's health drink into a pocket, clutched the bag of pastries between his teeth and stacked the two cups of coffee, leaving one hand free to open the door. If he walked into the reception area and found the ghost of a body swinging from the rafters he'd just leave the mess on the floor and walk out.

Charlie managed to open the door and made his way to the alarm panel...which had not been turned on. He'd have to talk to Declan about that.

As he headed to his new, probably haunted desk, he passed the stack of files he had left on the coffee table. He would put them away after he'd delivered Declan his drinks.

Charlie paused. Something was wrong. Everything was quiet. Declan always started his day by working out first thing in the morning. Charlie's pulse started to race. *What if...*

Charlie crept up the stairs far enough to peer into the apartment. Declan lay on his stomach, not moving, his head contorted to one side. Charlie waited for any sign that Declan was breathing. A gentle snort confirmed that Declan was still alive.

Charlie sat the coffees on the kitchen counter then pulled the health food drink out of his pocket. He opened the lid. The drink smelled repulsive. He snapped the lid back on, fished out a straw from his other pocket and drove it through the sticker on the top.

Maybe it tastes better than it smells.

He took a tiny sip and gagged.

Declan began to stir. Charlie moved closer. The sheets on the bed had been pushed aside exposing Declan's bare right leg and muscular buttock. Charlie considered bending down to kiss that mountain of muscle, but he had learned not to startle Declan when he was asleep. A week ago, an amorous kiss to Declan's inner thigh had resulted in Charlie being propelled through the air, luckily into a pile of laundry. Declan wasn't used to having someone around, and in his half-asleep state, had taken the tender caress as an attempt on his life. He was getting better with time, but it was clear that Declan had to be woken up very gently.

Before Charlie woke him up, he leaned in close and said, "Good morning, man I love. Are you awake?"

One eye of the muscled mountain opened. "Mumph."

"Up late?" Charlie asked.

Declan shifted a bit and winced. "Didn't you get my text? Since you weren't here, I stayed late at Bar-None last night."

Charlie smiled. He hadn't received the text. Declan had probably typed it and forgotten to press 'send'.

Declan hoisted himself up on one elbow. "I'm beginning to think that place might not be good for me. I'm getting too old for bar life."

"You're not *that* old," Charlie said, snuggling up to him. "It's just a hangover."

Declan hoisted himself around and landed his feet on the floor. His body was now wrapped in the top sheet making Declan look like he was wearing an ill-fitting toga. He stared groggily at Charlie.

"Here," Charlie said, passing him the smoothie. Declan had a long sip on the straw and sighed.

Charlie scowled. "I have no idea what's in that, but it made me gag when I tried it."

Declan looked at him in disbelief. "You sipped from my straw?"

"Yeah. And it tastes like ogre snot."

"You should never sip from another guy's straw."

Charlie was amused. The guy who could fish a dead body out of a swamp—or so Charlie had read in an early news report—was actually grossed out by sharing a drinking straw. "You've never complained about me putting your things in my mouth before."

"But...it's my straw..."

Charlie rubbed Declan's back. "Well, then don't use the straw. Coffee's on the counter. I'm heading downstairs to tidy up. Mrs Beckerman comes in today and I want everything perfect for her."

Charlie leaned over, gave Declan a kiss on the head then headed back down the stairs. He went to the car and retrieved his personal laptop, then returned to his desk where he spent the next thirty minutes getting it to talk to the office's Wi-Fi and printer. He'd have to ask Declan if they had money to buy him a new work computer now that Mrs Beckerman would be using the other one. Charlie also didn't have a phone for his desk. For now he could just use his cell phone. What if Mrs Beckerman got a call for him? He programmed his cell number into the main office phone on her desk so she could easily transfer any calls. She probably had her own way of doing things, but since she'd been away, he had implemented a number of changes to things like passwords and security codes. He wondered if she'd approve. The more Charlie thought about Mrs Beckerman's return, the more nervous he became.

As if on cue, she walked into the room. She was bundled in a winter coat and carried a large, black bag, looking like a very serious Mary Poppins.

"Good morning, Charlie," she said in a perfunctory voice, then headed into the kitchenette.

Mrs Beckerman returned without her coat. She was wearing a dark-grey business suit. "First things first," she said as she dropped her bag onto her chair, then reached in and pulled out a large handful of magazines. She marched toward the coffee table. Charlie realised too late that he'd forgotten to deal with the stack of files. She fanned out the new magazines, then picked up the old ones along with the files. She strode back to her desk, dumping the outdated periodicals noisily into the recycle bin. "There," she said, with a determined look on her face. "Better already."

As she set the files down on her desk, she looked toward where Charlie was sitting. "I see you've been busy. Very nice-looking office you've made for yourself."

"Uh, thanks. Can I get you a coffee?" he said, standing up and moving toward her.

"Thank you, Charlie, but that won't be necessary. Fetching coffee is *my* job now."

"Oh. Right. Sorry."

She opened a desk drawer and pulled out a mass of loose electronics cables. She held them out to Charlie.

"Sorry. Let me take those," he muttered.

Mrs Beckerman closed the drawer and began to adjust the chair to suit her. Charlie resisted the urge to explain how the chair worked. She looked up. "Why are you staring at me?"

"Oh, sorry. I just thought, if you had any questions..."

She gave him a withering glance.

"I'll just be over here if you need anything." He slunk back to his chair and busied himself on his computer. He pulled up the report on the Simon Griffin interview and reviewed his notes.

"Charlie?"

Charlie jumped. Mrs Beckerman was standing at his desk. How could she move so quietly?

"My, you are a skittish one," she said. "About the filing you didn't get around to — would you like to keep the files on *your* cases in *your* filing cabinet, or in with the main office files with Declan's?"

"Which would be best for you?" he asked cautiously.

"I think you're more than capable of handling your own files. And that way, they'll be at arm's reach and I'll have less filing to do," she said.

Mrs Beckerman handed him the slim folder containing the Chipping files. "Now — is there anything you need from me right now or can I get on with filing?"

"No, ma'am."

"Charlie — no need to be formal. We'll be working together. You can call me Mrs B."

"Thanks... Mrs B."

She headed back to her desk.

Charlie sorted out all of the old cables she'd given him, then labelled them and stowed them in the bottom drawer of his filing cabinet. He moved all of the security system manuals out of the cupboard in the kitchenette and organised them in his bookcase. When he glanced up, Mrs B was smiling at him.

"You remind me so much of Declan when he was first starting out. Eager to look professional. When I first met him, he was terrified that someone would expose him as a complete novice when it came to running the business. I told him from the word go it was clear he needed help and *I* was the person to help him. I don't think he even offered me the job. I just took it."

"You're kidding?"

"It's true. I like to think of myself as a good judge of people, and in spite of the fact he was so nervous, he treated me with kindness and respect. I knew he was a good person."

Charlie just nodded his head.

"My instinct says the same about you. We're going to get along just fine, Charlie Watts."

Charlie breathed a sigh of relief and his shoulders relaxed.

"Now, if you'll kindly tell me where my computer password Post-It note has gone…"

Charlie ran over to her desk with a new Post-It note that said 'WelcomeBackMrsB5%'. "This will be more than secure enough and save you time."

"Thank you."

Just then Declan descended the stairs from above and poked his head out from the inner office. "I hope you're playing fair, Mrs. B."

She smiled, but didn't say a word.

Declan turned to Charlie and said in a serious tone, "Can you come into my office? We need to talk about your interview with Simon Griffin."

Charlie smiled weakly. "Sure."

Why do I feel like I've done something wrong?

Chapter Thirteen

Declan sat down behind his desk and Charlie took the chair opposite.

Declan nodded his head toward the closed door, then said in a quiet voice, "So, how's it going out there?"

"Pretty well," Charlie replied.

"Interesting, because when Mrs B and I started to work together, that woman terrified me."

Charlie let out a long breath. "So, it's not just me. I think it's those laser-beam eyes of hers."

"Ahhh, then you've already experienced the power of the Beckerman stare."

"Yup."

They both laughed.

"It's humbling," Declan said. "But you'll get used to it and you'll learn to appreciate her and her skills."

"I hope it doesn't take too long," Charlie replied.

"You'll be fine. Now, let's talk about Simon Griffin. I read your report. What's your gut feeling about the guy?"

"Well, on the surface he seems nice enough. He has tons of money, in assets if not cash—his house in Banff is worth millions. But something feels off."

Declan leaned in. "What's that?"

"The note—it said 'I know what you did'. Simon said he had no idea what that meant, but I feel like he wasn't telling the truth."

"Okay. It's important to trust your gut. What else?"

Charlie furrowed his brow. "The note Simon gave me was signed 'Milo'. It's not exactly a common name and it's come up twice in the same week. Do you think it has anything to do with what Archie Whitcher said?"

"That's what I'm hoping to find out."

Charlie nodded. "So, you're going to take Mr Griffin's case?"

"Nope."

"Why not?"

"This thing with his kid—it's a missing persons case."

"So?" Charlie said.

"Well, most of the initial work will probably be computer searches, reviewing the existing interviews taken by the police, tracking down the mother and finding the name of Milo's friend. I don't think this is a case for me…but…I think it would be a perfect one for *you* to take on. It's time you tried something more substantial."

"*What?*" Charlie shouted. "I'm not fully licensed yet. Griffin came looking for you, not me. *You're* the detective!"

Declan smiled. "You're the one he opened up to. Everything you need to do, you've already done. You formed a bond with the man and you have a special knack for gathering information. I've seen you do it. Look at the Malcolm Tull case. You tracked down all of the people he'd been in contact with online, even though they were buried deep in false identities. This is what you were born to do."

Charlie sat in silence.

"Look, if you're worried, we can sit down and talk through anything you're not sure of, but we should definitely take the case. We need the money now that we have an extra mouth to feed," Declan said, nodding his head toward the outer office.

He moved around the desk and took the chair beside Charlie. "Archie Whitcher was trying to tell me something. I don't know what it all means, but I can't get it out of my head, and you know how discovering Freddy's body fucked me around. I feel like I owe it to the kid to see if something was missed. That's got to be my focus for the next few days."

Declan glanced over to the photograph of Freddy. "And, by the way, if you find Milo, I'm going to have a few questions for him."

Charlie stood. "All right. I'll do it. But would you at least call Simon and explain why you're sending your tech guy out to take over the search for his son?"

"You're not just the tech guy. You've got your own office now — well, sort of. I'll let him know that there's no one better in this firm to do the job."

Declan stood up and opened the door. "Mrs B, can you come in here for a sec?"

She entered, pad and pen at the ready.

Declan began. "The next little while will be baptism by fire for all of us. Mrs B, Charlie'll be your go-to-guy when it comes to anything tech, including the security system, which lately has become essential."

"Mysterious, but good to know," she said, smiling at Charlie.

"Charlie's also been thrown head-first into what could be a big money-making case for the firm. Mrs B, whatever support he needs, give it to him. Oh, and if a Tyler Chipping phones or comes around, direct him to me, no matter what. Chipping has a hate-on for Charlie and I don't want the guy anywhere near him."

"Understood," she said. "Charlie, do you have a photo of him you can pass on to me?"

"You bet."

"Good," she replied.

Declan sat for a moment looking at the two of them before Mrs B broke the silence.

"Aren't you going to say 'Dismissed'?"

"Why? You already did," Declan said.

Mrs B walked out of the room, but Charlie lingered. "Will you have time to call Simon this morning?"

"I promise," Declan said, raising three fingers in a Boy Scout salute. "I'll do it right now."

"Great."

Charlie left the office, closing the door behind him.

Declan dialled Simon's number. After a few rings it was answered. "Griffin residence. How may I help you?"

"May I speak to Simon Griffin, please? My name is Declan Hunt and Mr Griffin is expecting my call."

"One moment, please."

"Mr Hunt," a voice said over the phone. "Simon Griffin here. Thank you for getting back to me."

"I'm sorry it took a few days," Declan replied. "I've been a bit tied up."

"A man in demand is exactly who I'm looking for. It confirms your reputation as someone who knows what he's doing."

"Thank you," Declan said. "Now, I've looked over the file and Declan Hunt Investigations is interested in working with you to find your missing son. I've assigned the case to Charlie Watts. He handled your intake interview."

"He's quite young, isn't he?"

"Exactly, and that's the kind of person you need. Mr Watts can track people through even the faintest presence on the internet. He can also access police records in ways that most people cannot and he's not afraid to get his hands dirty. In short, Charlie is a tech and research genius and those are the types of skills you're going to need to find Milo. How do you feel about that?"

After a brief pause, Simon responded, "Yes. I quite liked Mr Watts. A bright young fellow. I think you're right. That's the best kind of man to go with in this digital age. So, what's the next step?"

"My secretary will email you a digital contract to sign. Once that's done, Charlie will be in touch."

"Excellent. I look forward to his call."

Declan disconnected and headed out to Charlie's desk. "It's all set."

"Great," Charlie said as his cell phone started to ring. "Mrs B, I'll give you Simon Griffin's contact information. Would you please prepare a contract and send it to him as soon as you can?"

She nodded.

Charlie looked at his phone's caller ID, smiled, and answered, "Declan Hunt Investigations. Charlie Watts speaking."

The person on the other end of the line spoke at length and Charlie's hands began to shake.

"Okay... Can I call you back?" Charlie clumsily disconnected from the call. The colour had drained from his face.

"What's wrong?" Declan asked.

"That was Carrie. Gran's in the hospital. She fell. She's...unconscious."

Declan went for his coat. "Come on. I'll take you over."

"No. No I... I've got to start on the case. It's important."

Mrs B looked toward Declan then intervened. "Well, you can't start the case until the contract is signed, and I've still got a *lot* of filing to do before it can be sent."

"Okay," Charlie replied uncertainly. He slowly stood.

"I'll take you," Declan said. "You're in no state to drive."

"No. I'll just get an Uber."

Declan frowned. "Are you sure you don't want me there?"

"I do, but...my folks'll be there. I haven't talked to them in a while and they don't know about us. They think you're just my boss and things could get awkward. My dad blames you for everything — wasting my degree, getting a job that got me beat up and hit by a car... I just don't think it'd be a good idea."

Mrs B looked at Declan. "Let the boy go on his own. He'll be fine."

Charlie put his hand on Declan's shoulder. "Never think that I don't want you with me. It's just that…"

"I understand," Declan said, kissing Charlie on the forehead. "You're doing what's right for you. Come on. Grab your coat and I'll take you down and get you an Uber."

Charlie picked up his phone and placed a call. "Carrie, I'll meet you at the hospital. I'll be there as soon as I can."

* * * *

As Charlie rode in the back of the car, he thought about Gran. She was more than just his grandmother — she knew his secrets. She was the only one in the family who knew he was gay and she didn't care. She loved him for who he was.

But when Charlie had started working with Declan, then moved in with Carrie, he'd abandoned his grandmother. How long had it been since he'd last seen her? Months. And when had he last called her? He couldn't remember. All because he'd become so wrapped up in his life. In Declan's life. And now she was in hospital, and he wasn't sure if she was going to make it.

Why was it that every time he took a step forward in his life, he felt like he was always moving in the wrong direction?

Chapter Fourteen

Charlie held onto Carrie's hand for support. He took a deep breath and entered the hospital. They were directed to a private room just off the ER. Charlie's parents, Maggie and Ted, were on the opposite side of the room. When she saw Charlie, his mom walked around the bed and put her arms around him.

His father just said, "It's good you're here, Charlie. And nice to see you, too, Carrie."

It had been a long time since he'd seen his parents.

Charlie made his way to the bedside.

Gran was lying with her eyes closed, hands at her side. Her right wrist was splinted. Tubes and cables ran from her arms to a series of machines. She looked…

"Am I too late?" he squeaked out, his eyes filling with tears.

"You think I'd go without saying goodbye?" a voice said. He looked down at Gran and she opened her eyes. "Lean down and give your gran a kiss."

He did what he was told, then slid his arms around her and gave her a gentle hug.

"I love you, Gran," he whispered to her.

"I love you too, boy."

"What happened?"

"Oh, you know me. Always causing trouble. I was just heading to the bathroom when I felt dizzy. Next thing I know," she said, pointing to the monitors beside the bed, "I'm here hooked up to all these gizmos."

"Your gran fell and broke her wrist," his father added. "The doctor told us they'll get her in for surgery and deal with that, but they're running some tests to see why she lost consciousness."

A nurse walked in and took Gran's vitals. Charlie gently rubbed Gran's shoulder. "Is it serious, nurse?"

The nurse turned his attention to Gran. "We're still waiting for the results of your blood work. Then I think they're scheduling a CT scan just to rule out anything up here," he said, tapping his head, "which might have caused your blackout. The good news is your vitals are stable, but we still have to get that wrist looked after. The surgeon will be in to see you shortly."

The nurse headed out of the room.

Charlie grabbed Gran's good hand. "Sorry I haven't been around lately."

"I know you've been busy. Still in the detective business?" she asked.

"I am."

"Good. Good for you."

"I got a promotion," he said with a grin.

"Wonderful! I hope it includes benefits." The slight smile on her lips said volumes. She knew he was seeing Declan outside of work.

Charlie's mother interrupted the conversation. "I hope Charlie's been no bother for you, Carrie."

"I have to tell you, Mrs Watts, it's been so nice having him live with me. We had a great time over the weekend shopping for some new furniture and knickknacks for the place."

"Oh?"

Charlie's mother's eyes lit up. "Are you two planning on moving into a bigger place?"

"No, Mother," he said firmly.

Gran spoke up. "Could I talk to Charlie in private, please? It's important."

Carrie looked at Gran, then Maggie and Ted. "Why don't I take you to the cafeteria for a coffee? I can tell you all about what we bought for our place."

Carrie dragged Ted and Maggie out of the room.

Gran chuckled. "I swear they won't be happy until you and Carrie get married and have a child. I think they'd even settle for just the latter."

"A child out of wedlock?" Charlie gasped in mock horror. "What will the neighbours think?"

"Ah, Charlie. I've missed you. So, tell me. How's your life with your detective going?"

"I think everything is going fine."

"Still mad about him, then?" Gran asked.

"Mad, and frustrated."

"Well, life isn't always like a fairy tale."

"With me, Gran, it's always a fairy tale."

A broad smile filled her face.

"Glad you haven't lost your sense of humour. I'd love to meet your detective some time. From what you've told me, I think I'd like him."

"I know he'd love you. I'll just have to find a time when Mom and Dad aren't around so we can actually talk."

"Well, you can bring him around here when they're gone, but you know what, Charlie? This fall has made me realise that I won't be around forever. And I'd love it if, before I die, I could see you truly happy."

"What do you mean?" Charlie asked.

"You need to tell your parents the truth so you can live your life on your own terms. You're a grown man. I hate to see you putting a wedge between us all because you feel you can't be honest with them."

"I'm not sure if I can," Charlie replied.

"If it helps, I think Maggie might suspect. And don't give me that look. I said nothing, but she's your mother and she's not blind. She probably noticed that starry-eyed look that you got when Declan's name came up in conversation. And she did see that picture you sent to me — the one of you and Declan all dressed up in your tuxedos going to that fancy party."

"Does my father know?"

"He hasn't quite gotten over the fact you don't play hockey with him anymore. I don't think he's expecting the news that his son is gay, but, he'll come around when he has to face up to it. If nothing else, he's my son and he'll listen to me. Just let me know what I can do to make this work out," Gran continued. "I could always tell them it's my dying wish to see my only grandson happy. They wouldn't dare stand in the way of that! Promise me you'll do this before I die."

He looked her straight in the eye. "I promise, Gran, as long as you promise me you won't die anytime soon."

She smiled. "It's a deal. Now, tell me all about your latest case."

Chapter Fifteen

When Declan got back from saying goodbye to Charlie, Mrs B was holding up a message. "It's from Katherine O'Grady. All she said was that she needed you to come to her place right now. Here's her number in case you don't have it."

Declan phoned Katherine, but she didn't pick up. He made his way down to his van and cleared the fresh snow off the windows and headlights then drove straight over. As he walked up to her house he noted that the driveway and the path to the front door had been recently shovelled. She must have been clearing the walks when he'd called back.

Declan knocked on the door. He heard nothing. A minute later, the living room drapes shifted. He knocked again. This time the lace curtain on the window in the front door moved a bit. Declan briefly caught an eye peering out. There was the sound of a deadbolt being drawn back and the door opened as much as it could with the chain guard still in place.

"Are you alone?" she asked.

"Yes. What happened, Katherine?"

"Just a sec." She closed the door, disengaged the chain then opened the door wide.

"Take off your boots and come in quickly," she said, heading off to the kitchen. He followed her.

As they sat at the table she set out two glasses. "*Crème de menthe*?"

"Sure, but just a small one."

"I got your message," he said as she poured. "I was a bit worried when you didn't pick up the phone when I called back."

"To be truthful, I was a bit embarrassed after I left the message. Thought maybe I'd overreacted. But you're here now."

"Overreacted to what, Katherine?"

"There was a man watchin' Archie's house. He kept his distance at first, then I think he noticed me lookin' at him through the window."

"Had you seen him before?"

She nodded her head. "I'm sure it was the same guy that I saw on the street the day Archie was killed."

"Did you call the police?" Declan asked.

Katherine looked at him and cocked an eyebrow. "I called you. I don't trust the police." She took a swig of her drink.

"All right. Can you describe him?"

"Like I said the other day, about your height. He's an older man and a nice dresser. He had a long light-brown coat."

"There's nothing new in that," Declan said.

Katherine scowled. "Well, he was wrapped up in a brown scarf and dark glasses, if that helps. I just thought you'd wanna know that he'd been around again. And there's something else. Look, it might be nothing, but on the day that Archie was murdered, there was a car parked up the street I'd never seen before. It was an older car. Grey. I know everyone on the street, and it's not one of theirs."

"Did you see it today?" Declan asked.

"Nope. But that doesn't mean it might not belong to the man in the brown coat. Maybe this time he parked it a couple of blocks away so it wouldn't be noticed. Crooks do that, you know."

"Katherine, you're a one-woman neighbourhood watch."

"I should have thought of it before. I figured you might like to see a picture."

Declan's eyes widened. "You took a picture of the car?"

Katherine nodded. "Pure dumb luck. On the day Archie died, that car was parked under a burnt-out street light that I've been complainin' to the city about for weeks. I took the picture of the pole so I could report it for a repair. Then, after this morning's encounter I got to thinkin' about that car and the photo, and… Let me show you."

She opened up her phone and scrolled through a few pictures. "Ah, here it is."

Katherine turned the phone toward Declan and zoomed in on the car. It was an early 2000 model Chevy Impala. What was most significant was the licence plate — clearly visible.

"And that was parked there on the day of the murder?" he clarified.

She nodded.

"You didn't happen to get a picture of the man in the brown coat, did you?"

She rolled her eyes. "Don't be a smartass. But now that you say it, I wish I'd thought of it."

"Can you send me a copy of this picture?"

She passed him the phone. "You do it."

Declan found his number in her recent contacts and sent himself a text with the photo attached, then handed the phone back to her.

"It might be nothin'," Katherine said.

"Or it might be something important," Declan said. "I promise I'll check up on it for you. And if the man in the brown coat comes back...call the police. If he did have something to do with Archie's murder, they need to know about it."

Declan took a small sip of his drink. "I have to go, Katherine, but I'll let you know if I find out anything more."

Declan put on his shoes and headed back to his van. He should call the police with this, but it might be nothing and he wanted to check it out on his own first. Declan had connections that could run a plate and track down an address. And if it did turn out to be something important, he'd give Sawchuck a call. If nothing else, it gave him something to focus on until he heard back from Charlie.

Declan drove back to the office and walked slowly up the stairs. Mrs B was seated at her desk like she'd never been away. She looked up, "Charlie phoned and said he won't be in for a bit."

"Did he say how his grandmother is doing?"

"She's stable, but he sounded very concerned. You might want to reach out to him."

"I will," Declan replied. "By the way, did you send Simon Griffin's contract?"

"Yes, and he signed it back. A paper copy's in the folder in Charlie's filing cabinet."

"Good. Please email Mr Griffin and tell him that Charlie will be in contact with him in the near future once he's completed some preliminary work."

Mrs B gave Declan a hard stare.

"Don't give me that look. If Charlie's not back in a few days, I'll start digging into the case. But Charlie'll be back soon… I know it."

"You're the boss," she replied.

Declan went into his office and closed the door. He pulled out his phone and texted Charlie.

Take as much time off as you need.

He hit 'send', then realised he probably shouldn't have mentioned work at all.

He texted again.

If there's anything you need, just ask. Wish I could be there with you.

He hit 'send' then reread his text and groaned. The wording of the second part of the text might make Charlie feel guilty about asking him not to come with him in the first place. Charlie would have known exactly what to say at a moment like this. Declan thought about sending a third text, but knew he'd just dig himself a deeper hole. He tossed his phone on the desk, then went to the credenza and poured himself a scotch.

Keep it together, Hunt. No matter how much you love him, you've still got a business to run.

Chapter Sixteen

It was late in the afternoon and Simon dozed in his chair. He hadn't slept well the previous night. He rarely slept well these days and this Milo business had left him feeling unsettled.

He went into his office and distracted himself at his desk. In the so-called good old days, he would have buried himself in work. But work, as it stood now, came in drips and dribbles. It was an insult. He had climbed the ladder to the highest rungs of Monarch Holdings, a place he'd focused his energies on for most of his adult life. He'd been invaluable to them and he deserved to be promoted to the top spot, once that position was available — when the inevitable happened to Harlen Feist.

As he pondered the past, his thoughts were interrupted by Jasmine. She carried an oversized package in her arms.

"I think you've been waiting for this," she said with a smile.

In fact, Simon had been waiting for this package for over six months. Negotiations for the acquisition of the package's contents had been ongoing for over a decade. The owner had not wanted to part with it, but Simon knew how much of a financial bind the seller was in. He could have bartered the man down on the sale price, but he chose not to. He respected the seller. He and Simon had much in common, most of all a love of history. Besides, if Simon didn't buy it, the seller would have to go into the open to unload it, and that would be the last thing the man would want to do. The powers that be who would have swept in to grab it would have only given the seller a fraction of what it was really worth.

Simon carefully slit the sealing tape which closed the heavy corrugated cardboard box. Inside, surrounded by foam packing peanuts, lay another box. The contents were packed layer within layer, like a *matryoshka* doll, in order to protect what lay at the core.

As Simon extracted the inner box, the packing peanuts spilled all over his desk, but the normally fastidious Simon didn't care. He was frantic to discover what was inside.

He carefully opened the inner package and saw two small, grip-seal bags. He had trouble deciding which to open first. Simon chose the one with the shiniest appearance.

His hands shook as he pried apart the sealed bag. He put on a pair of clean cotton gloves then slid the contents into his hand. The seventh-century circular gilt-copper brooch with an inlay of garnets and delicate shell discs was no more than two centimetres wide. It was one of the original finds collected from the Anglo-Saxon burial mounds of Sutton Hoo in Suffolk,

England. Simon was fascinated by anything related to burial practices, but this rare piece had just become the Hope Diamond of his collection. And it was legal—technically. As long as no one asked the British Museum.

While the contents of the second bag paled in comparison to the first in the looks department, they thrilled Simon just as much. The bag, which would remain closed, looked as though it contained mainly sand and coarse grit. But visible through the clear plastic were large pieces of shell-like material. Simon looked at them through his jeweller's loupe. His heart pounded. These were fragments of bone of the very man who had worn the brooch.

He placed the bags back within the small box and reverently walked them to the bookcase across the room. He pulled on the first edition of Howard Carter's memoir *The Tomb of Tutankhamen*. There was the comforting click of a latch and the bookcase swung outward, revealing the door of a large walk-in vault with an old-fashioned set of tumbler locks. This was where he kept his treasures.

The vault had been one of Milo's favourite places in the house. Even at an early age, he was allowed to go in and look at daddy's treasures as long as Simon was there and Milo didn't touch anything. Like his father, Milo was fascinated by the stories associated with the collection of burial treasures.

Simon couldn't help but wonder what Milo would have thought of his new acquisitions.

Milo. No matter how Simon tried to distract himself, things these days always came back to Milo. Was he really alive, or was it just a sick joke? And if it wasn't a sick joke… Simon had to find him, and quickly. There were things they needed to discuss. Hopefully Tom was right about Declan Hunt and his firm.

He picked up the phone and placed a call.

* * * *

Tom Semple lived alone in a two-bedroom condo in the Beltline district in Calgary—most of the time. Sometimes he stayed at Simon's house, but only when there was business to take care of at The Paddock, and clearly there was business tonight.

Tom ran over the current problem. Simon had called and he was in a tailspin over this whole Milo business. It was interesting. Simon hadn't even particularly liked the kid. He had certainly never expressed love for him. For the most part, Simon was all business and Milo was, well, Milo was just a kid. The only thing they'd had in common were antiquities. Both had spent hours looking over Simon's collection, but aside from that, they hadn't spent much time together.

Milo certainly hadn't talked to his father about the fact he was gay. Jasmine, the housekeeper, knew. So did Tom, but he wasn't bothered by it—that would be hypocritical. He didn't give a shit about who Milo was attracted to as long as he didn't go bringing strangers into the house. There were rules at The Paddock.

Simon's recent preoccupation with Milo's disappearance had resulted in Tom making a difficult choice. He'd suggested an outsider. He knew Simon wouldn't say anything that would compromise the business, and, by reputation, Declan Hunt was a fucking Boy Scout when it came to honour and discretion. He could be useful. Very useful indeed.

Tom needed to find out who had sent Simon the message. But there was another reason to use Declan. Tom wasn't able to call on his usual resources. If Monarch found out about the note and anything led back to Tom, it could cost him everything...possibly even his life. Instead, he would let Declan do the legwork and once the detective had found the person that had sent the note, Tom would take action. He'd already done a little checking on his own, but so far that had been a dead end.

When Simon had called Tom, he'd suggested they meet for supper at The Azure Owl in Canmore. For Simon it was only a fifteen-minute drive, but for Tom it was over an hour...in good weather. But since Simon paid all the bills, Tom didn't argue.

He gave himself plenty of time to get there. A Chinook wind from the west had raised the temperature by twenty degrees, melting the snow off of the roads. Even so, the traffic was bad and Tom arrived just in time. He pulled into the lot, parked next to Simon's prized Bentley then made his way in.

"Mr Griffin's table, please," he said to the hostess who was dressed in a skin-tight, floor-length dress. It might as well have been made of body paint. He could see...everything.

"Simon," he said, extending his hand as the painted woman pulled out his chair, then seamlessly tucked it under him as he sat.

Simon shook Tom's hand, then waved down their server. His name tag identified him as Wolf. He was a handsome man in his twenties. "A scotch, neat, for my friend. Same as mine."

The server nodded and left without a word. Tom admired the view as the server walked away from him.

"More to your taste than the hostess?" Simon asked.

"He's a little young, but he'd do in a pinch. So, to what do I owe the pleasure of this dinner?" Tom asked.

Simon sipped at his drink. "I wanted to thank you for your help. I signed the contract with that fellow you recommended. I think his firm is just what we need to find Milo or, at least whoever is pretending to be him."

"Good," Tom said.

Simon settled back into his chair. "But it won't be Declan handling the case. I went to the office and the young man who I spoke to will be doing the work. His name is Charlie Watts and apparently he's highly skilled at finding people."

"I referred you to Declan," Tom said, more sternly than he'd meant to. "How do you know this Charlie guy can be trusted?"

"I signed a non-disclosure agreement and Declan himself personally assured me that I'm in good hands. I know the stakes are high, but sometimes, you've just got to follow your gut."

"Follow your gut? I wish I'd been there when you had your meeting."

"Tom, we need fresh young eyes on this," Simon said with a cold edge to his voice. "Don't forget, you had ten years to find Milo, and nothing. Be grateful I took your advice in the first place. This is a huge risk, and for both of our sakes, I hope it works out. Do you understand?"

Tom gritted his teeth and nodded.

Wolf returned and silently placed Tom's scotch on the table.

Simon smiled and turned to the server. "So Wolf, my *gut instinct* says that the *filet mignon* special tonight would be an excellent choice, but my companion doesn't always trust my instincts. What do you think?"

"It's an excellent choice sir," Wolf replied.

"Wonderful," Simon said. "We'll *both* have the *filet mignon*. Rare."

The waiter took the order and left the two alone.

"Now," Simon continued, "let's talk about something else. You might be interested in hearing about my most recent acquisitions."

* * * *

The rest of the dinner was without incident. It appeared to Tom, that for Simon, fences between old friends could be mended as quickly as they were broken. The bill was paid and the handsome server Wolf was left a hefty tip.

Tom and Simon left the restaurant and walked toward their cars. As they rounded the corner of the building, Simon stopped dead in his tracks. He looked as if he had seen a ghost. Simon slowly raised his hand and pointed at his car. There was a letter 'M' crudely gouged into the driver-side of his beloved Bentley.

Simon let loose an unholy cry.

"Whoever it is, I'll kill him!" he yelled out. "I'll find him and I swear I will tear him to shreds."

Tom moved closer. Something was tucked under the windshield wiper. It was a piece of paper. He carefully extracted and unfolded a printed message.

Everything of value will be taken away from you.
It's time for the truth to come out.
I'm watching you.

Simon snatched the paper from Tom's hand.

It was then that Tom noticed a piece of paper on *his* windshield. He opened it.

I know what you did!

Simon pulled out his phone and started to place a call.

"What are you doing?" Tom demanded.

"I'm calling Monarch."

Tom tore the phone from Simon's hands. "You can't. Don't do anything you'll regret. Now is not the time to act rashly." Tom took a deep breath. "Look — the car can be repaired easily enough. This" — he held up the notes — "this is something entirely different. I'll follow you home and we'll discuss what to do about these. But Monarch cannot know about this."

Simon nodded his head and got into his car.

As Tom followed Simon back to The Paddock, one thought kept rolling around in his head — *I need to take control.*

Chapter Seventeen

Declan woke up and didn't feel like working out. He sat on the edge of his bed and stretched. *Is this it?* he thought. *The beginning of the slide into old age and all it holds – withered biceps and a paunch.*

He looked over to the other side of the bed where Charlie hadn't slept for the past four nights, having spent the weekend with Carrie and not returning from the hospital last night. Declan checked his phone but there were no new messages. He sent a quick text.

Thinking about you. I miss you. Call me.

Declan headed downstairs into the kitchenette and made himself a coffee. He prepped the drip machine for Mrs B then returned to the main room and glanced at the time. Eight-twenty-five. Declan deactivated the door alarm. Charlie would be impressed he'd remembered to set it in the first place. He reminded himself that either he, or Charlie, had to show Mrs B how it worked.

As Declan plopped himself down on the couch, he glanced at *Rocky Mountain Leisure*, one of the new magazines Mrs B had brought in. He couldn't remember the last time he'd just taken some time for himself like this. A cup of coffee, a magazine and nothing else.

Declan picked up the glossy tourist publication and flipped through the pages. The first article he came across was on Banff. There were the obligatory photos of Sulphur Mountain and the hot springs, ski lifts and cable cars, and the Banff Springs Hotel — then a picture of a beautiful old private home on Buffalo Avenue.

A rare example of mountain architecture from the mid-20th century, the prestigious home of Simon Griffin graces the shores of the Bow River. Rumours have it that he used the home to woo former film star Michelle Coleman...

His reading was disrupted by the sound of the street-level door chime and footsteps climbing the stairs. The office door opened and in walked —

"Charlie!" Declan shouted.

"I'm back," Charlie said, before running over to Declan, who stood and gathered him up in his arms.

"I couldn't sleep last night," Charlie whispered. "I couldn't get you out of my mind."

"Me too," Declan replied, nuzzling his nose into Charlie's mop of hair.

"I'm sorry about yesterday," Charlie murmured, "about not letting you come with me."

"It's okay, I understand." *Partially*, Declan thought to himself. "I think you made a logical decision."

Charlie pushed away and looked Declan in the eye. "No! You're part of my life now and if my parents can't handle it, well…I'll have to figure out what to do about that…eventually."

Declan nodded. "I know you'll do what's right." He kissed Charlie. "So how's your gran?"

"She's a fighter — I'll give her that. It turns out she fainted because she was dehydrated. When she took her tumble, she broke her wrist, which isn't great, but she promised me that she wasn't going to let it slow her down for long."

"Still sounds pretty serious," Declan said. "How long's she going to be in the hospital?"

"Once her bloodwork comes back clean, and as long as her vitals are stable, she'll be okay to go home. They thought in a day or two. So what did I miss? I'm ready to get back to work."

Declan raised an eyebrow. "Are you sure? If you need more time off — "

Charlie interrupted, "No. When I saw Gran lying there in bed, with tubes and wires coming out of her…I realised that that could be any of us at any time. One silly move can change everything in an instant. I don't want to be the guy who realises too late in the game that he missed out on what he wanted to do with his life because he was too slow, or too afraid to do something. I want it all — the job, my family…and you. It doesn't all have to happen at once. Or maybe it will. I don't know. But what I do know is that I need to get back to work."

Declan smiled. "When did you get to be so smart? Did they teach that to you at university?"

"No. I just picked it up from watching the old people I hang with," he said, winking.

"Okay," Declan said. "Let me fill you in on what's happened since you left yesterday morning. Simon signed the contract, so you can start working on the case. And in other news, I found out about a strange car that was spotted on the street near Archie's place on the day of the murder."

"Oh?"

"And Katherine took a picture of it, along with the licence plate. I'm in the process of tracking the registration."

"Holy crap," Charlie said. "That's amazing."

Declan continued. "It may be a dead end but...maybe not. The other thing I found out was the guy who Katherine saw on the street on the day of the murder, she spotted him again on the street yesterday. Katherine said that he was in an expensive long, light-brown coat and looked like a stylish gangster. I think I should let the police know to keep an eye on her. So, why don't you start digging into Milo? Work your social media magic. Dig up anything you can on Simon, and Milo's mother, too. I read in your report that her name was Michelle Coleman. She's mentioned in one of the new magazines Mrs B brought in. Maybe Milo's been in touch with his mom."

"I'm on it," Charlie said. "And what are you going to do?"

"I'm going to give Gary a heads-up on Katherine's visitor, then call a friend of mine at the Alberta Motor Association and see who that licence plate belongs to."

Chapter Eighteen

It was just after one when Charlie picked up the phone and called Simon.

"Good afternoon — Griffin residence."

"Good afternoon. My name is Charlie Watts. I'm calling from Declan Hunt Investigations. May I speak with Mr Griffin, please?"

"One moment please," the voice said.

After a short pause Simon came on the line. "Charlie. Good to hear from you again. Don't tell me you're calling with good news so soon?"

"No, I'm afraid not, Mr Griffin. I'm just calling with a few requests. Would you be able to email me the most recent picture of Milo that you have?"

"I can send you a scan of an old photo if you'd like. I'll get that to you as soon as I get off the phone. It's a nice picture. I'm sure you'll like it."

"Great. You can just send it to the email address on the contract. Our office manager will keep her eye open for it and get it to me as soon as it comes in."

Charlie glanced over toward Mrs B who sat at her desk with an unreadable look on her face.

"Sorry," he whispered in her direction.

"One other thing, Mr Griffin. When you were in to see me the other day, we had spoken about getting the contact information for your ex-wife. Would you have that handy by any chance?"

There was a long silence on the other end of the line.

"Yes," Simon said, "I have it here, somewhere. Just a minute."

There was a clunk as Simon put the phone down. Charlie played a game of 'name that noise'. He definitely heard the sound of a metal filing drawer being opened.

As Charlie stood and stretched, Mrs B called out, "Can I make you a coffee? I'm getting one for myself."

"Latte, please," he whispered.

Mrs B got up and headed toward the stairs. "Sounds like a job for Gwen."

"I don't want you to go to any trouble."

"Not a problem. I need the exercise," she said, heading out.

"Found it!" a voice bellowed into his ear. "I'd filed it under 'D' for Divorce. We haven't been in touch for a long time, Charlie. I'm not sure if she's still there." He quickly rattled off an address in Laguna Beach, California.

"Thanks, Mr Griffin. I'll keep you informed on how things are going. Just one last thing. I've been thinking a lot about that note, and the part that said 'I know what you did'—you're sure you have no idea what that might be referring to?"

There was a pause on the line, then Simon replied, "No. But I'll give it some thought, Charlie, and let you know if I think of anything."

"All right, Mr Griffin. I'll be in touch soon."

As Charlie disconnected, he scowled. That pause... Simon definitely wasn't telling him something. He'd have to ponder that later but he had other work to do in the meantime.

Charlie started to search for the software he'd need to take the photo image of Milo and turn it from a mid-teen to someone that might be recognisable today. His research led him to a highly recommended app called BenButton, obviously named after Benjamin Button, the character from the movie who aged in reverse. Apparently, the app worked well in both directions. He installed the software.

Next he did a basic search on the words 'Milo', 'Banff' and 'Griffin' and turned up nothing of value. Surprisingly, there wasn't anything on Milo going missing ten years ago. Charlie knew that the police had classified the boy as a runaway, but he still found it strange that there was no mention online.

Then Charlie did an extensive search on 'Simon Griffin' to find out if there had been any threats toward him that had hit the media. Other than Banff locals mouthing off about him being a rich guy occupying a property that should be turned over to the park — there was nothing. As for what he was worth — one online site estimated his net worth was in the neighbourhood of twenty-five to thirty-five million. Charlie was surprised that there wasn't more bad press on him. Rich people always had detractors.

Mrs B reappeared and handed Charlie his latte, and a bag.

"Gwen said you couldn't survive without these," she said, pointing to the bag which held two *pains au chocolat*.

"Here," he said, pulling out his wallet.

"Don't worry. I have a budget line for Gwen."

"Oh?"

"Don't tell me you never discovered *that* in the budget. We would have gone bankrupt on what Declan pays for americanos alone if I hadn't been able to write it off as 'research fees'. Now, do you need anything else, Mr Big-Shot Detective?"

"No, thank you, Mrs B," Charlie said. The safest thing to do was to stay at his desk and get his research done. He still had to try to locate Michelle Coleman and he wanted to dig deeper into Simon's past, including his business dealings and his associates.

* * * *

Simon hung up the phone and sat at his desk staring into nothingness. He had been clenching his teeth — hard.

"Jasmine?" he yelled.

The housekeeper sauntered in. "Yes?"

He snapped his neck around. "Is Tom still here?"

"I believe he's upstairs, reading."

"Can you ask him to come down? We need to talk."

She said nothing, but nodded and left. A few moments later Tom entered the office and closed the door behind him.

"Has something happened?" he asked calmly.

"I just had a call from Charlie Watts, who was asking some interesting questions."

"Did you tell him about last night's attack?"

"No. Not yet, but his questions got me thinking."

"About?"

"The notes must be from Milo. He knew what that car meant to me. He knew damaging it would hurt me down to the very core of my being. And if Charlie does manage to locate Milo… I've been thinking…the night I last saw him, he said he knew what I'd done. Do you think it's possible he found out about what happened to Harlen Feist's son Roger all those years ago?"

Tom shook his head. "If that was true, he would have acted on that information sooner than now."

Simon walked over to the window and stared out at the mountains. "Well, if Milo does have any information on that untimely death, and that Watts kid finds him… I'm worried that perhaps I was hasty in hiring Declan Hunt Investigations. Do you think I should just tell Charlie that his services are no longer needed?"

Tom said, "No, not yet. No matter what, we have to find who ever sent the notes. We'll just let Charlie-boy know that he's only supposed to locate Milo and tell us where he can be found, but *no* contact with him should be made. I know one thing for sure—Monarch can't find out this is going on. It puts us at risk. We'll use the resources of the detective agency and once we locate the culprit, we'll take care of the problem ourselves. Nobody else has to know."

Simon paced the room, then stared intently at Tom. "I want you to keep an eye on Charlie Watts. I want to know where he's going and who he's talking to before he tells me. I trust you, Tom. I hope that trust hasn't been misplaced, but if it has, just remember, you're the one who suggested Hunt in the first place."

Chapter Nineteen

Mrs B cleared her throat. "I've just received an email from Simon Griffin. He says that if you find anything on Milo, that you should come to him first before taking any action."

"Got it," Charlie replied.

"He also sent the photo of his son that you requested."

"Can I see it please, Mrs B?"

She walked over to his desk and handed him a USB key. "Here. It's labelled 'Milo'. When you've got a few moments, you might want to set up your own corporate email address. It'll save me time."

"Thanks. I'll do that," he said sheepishly.

Charlie inserted the thumb drive into his computer and transferred the file to the Simon Griffin folder on his hard drive. He double-clicked on the file name and the image opened up. There he was — Milo.

Simon was right, it was a good picture. The teen stood on the banks of a river with the mountains behind him. He had a slim build and his curly light-brown hair cascaded off his head to well below his ears. His cheeks still carried a bit of baby fat, which rounded out his face. He looked like a professional model, but his dark-brown eyes gave off a sense of deep loneliness. Milo looked very little like his father.

Maybe he took after his mother.

Charlie opened the BenButton app and uploaded the image. He'd played with these programs before and was amazed at how 'imaginative' they could be, if software could be described as having an imagination. This program, however, utilised more advanced artificial intelligence.

Charlie followed the prompts, first identifying the year that the original image had been taken, as well as the age of the person depicted at the time. The program also asked what age he wanted the new image to represent, as well as other attributes including the current location, and the economic and social status of the person. That would affect things like clothing and hair style. He pressed the button labelled "Age me".

Within sixty seconds, the program offered up three options for what the Milo of today might look like. Charlie picked up his laptop and walked into Declan's office to show him the results. "I give you present-day Milo with three different looks," Charlie said, showing him the computer.

Declan's eyes widened. "Wow. These are great."

"I tested the software on a picture of me, ageing me back to when I was a kid, and it was pretty accurate. So hopefully it works as well when it makes people look older."

Declan stared at the pictures on Charlie's laptop, nodding. "Can you send me a copy of these? I think I'll take them over to Katherine O'Grady and see if any of them ring a bell." He looked up at Charlie. "Archie's last words were 'It was Milo'. Maybe she saw him."

"Or," Charlie offered, "maybe Milo was the mysterious man in the brown coat. I'll email them to you right away." Charlie took his computer back from Declan. "Now to see if internet searches can find anything that matches these pictures. I'll be at my desk if you need me."

"Great," Declan said, "Would you mind closing the door on your way out? I have a personal call to place."

"Sure."

Charlie left Declan's office wondering if Milo was, indeed, involved in Archie's murder. He also wondered who Declan was calling.

* * * *

As soon as Charlie had left the office, Declan picked up the phone. He found the number he needed in his contacts and called it.

"Hey," a voice answered. "Long time, no hear. Can I assume that you're not just calling to ask how my day's going? — which is deathly slow by the way."

Declan laughed. "No. Not this time, Martin. Are you still at the AMA? I have a professional favour to ask you."

"So not a booty call then?"

"No," Declan replied.

"I've seen the pictures in the paper of that cutie you've been seeing. Must be serious. The boys at the bathhouse were convinced that you'd died."

"Nope. Still alive."

"All right," Martin said. "And yes, I'm still at the AMA. What do you need?"

"I have to track down a licence plate. Gotta pen?" Declan asked.

"If it was anyone else, I'd say no," Martin admitted, "but for old times' sake and a few of the nights we spent together, I'll do it. Shoot."

Declan rhymed off the plate number.

"Got it," Martin said. "I'll run that licence number for you as soon as I can. I've got a few things to do first. Apparently, because they pay me, the AMA wants me to take care of their work first."

"I appreciate it. Talk to you later. Call me when you find out anything."

Declan hung up, then called Katherine O'Grady.

"You again," she answered.

Declan grinned. "Yup. The bad penny calls. Listen, I was thinking of popping by, if that's okay with you. I want to show you a picture and see if it looks familiar. Would you mind?"

"If it's somethin' from years gone by, I wouldn't count on it. My memory's not what it used to be, if it ever was in the first place."

"No," Declan assured her, "if you recognise this guy, you would have seen him recently."

"Mysterious, but sure. Come over whenever you want. I'm not goin' anywhere."

"I'll be there around two o'clock," Declan replied, then disconnected.

I hope this works…

He wasn't going to hold his breath, but he'd rather be surprised than not to have tried at all.

* * * *

For the third time, Declan stood in front of the door at Katherine's home and rang the doorbell. As he waited, he looked around. There was no sign of any police presence, but given that forensics would have wrapped up their work by now, there would be little more to discover at Archie's place...unless the murderer returned to the scene of the crime.

He heard a door close and the sound of feet crunching on snow. Katherine was making her way home from Archie's place.

"You know, if it would be easier for you, I could just rent you a room. The commute here must be tirin'," she said, squeezing past Declan and unlocking her front door.

"In case you were worried, I wasn't destroyin' evidence. I was just checkin' up on things over there. Just 'cause Archie's gone doesn't mean I can't take care of the house. I'm responsible for it as the executor of his will. Don't want the heat to go off and the pipes to freeze. I suppose you want to talk to me inside?"

"If it's okay with you."

"Boots off. Don't want muck tracked into my house."

Declan stepped in, removed his boots, and placed them on the tray by the closet. He hung his coat on the hook by the door and followed Katherine into the kitchen.

"I suppose you want a *crème de menthe*?" she asked.

"Love one. Thanks," he lied, settling into what had become his chair.

She smiled. "Don't know many men who like the drink. Good to find a kindred spirit."

She poured two small glasses. "To what do I owe the pleasure?"

Declan pulled out his phone. "I want you to have a look at a set of pictures of a guy and tell me if he looks familiar." He passed the phone over to Katherine. "Take your time. You can swipe right to see pictures two and three."

Katherine stared intently at the screen, flipping back and forth between images. She seemed to always return to the second picture. Whenever she was looking at it, she raised her eyebrows slightly.

Damn it if Charlie hasn't struck gold with that program of his.

"This one," she said, sliding the phone back to Declan.

"Are you sure?" Declan asked.

"You bet. I never missed that show, although I thought his character was a bit of a dick."

Declan had no idea what she was talking about.

"It's one of the kids from *Beverly Hills 90210*, isn't it? Do you know the guy?"

Declan took a deep breath. "The question is, do you? Have you seen this person anywhere around Archie's place?"

"Why would a guy from *Beverly Hills 90210* hang around Archie's place?"

"Never mind," he said. While he was tucking his phone back into his pocket he glanced over at the kitchen counter. There were two things that hadn't been there before — a framed photograph and a stuffed bear. He recognised both.

"Katherine…the picture and the bear over there," he said pointing to the counter. "Didn't they used to be in Archie's place?"

She glanced in their direction and cautiously answered, "Well…yeah."

"Why did you bring them over here?"

"You wouldn't believe me if I told you."

"Try me," he said.

Katherine walked over and gently picked the objects up, bringing them back to the table. "I know you don't believe there was a thread of humanity in Archie, but he really missed Freddy. That picture meant a lot to him. It was the only one where the boy's laughin'. I don't even know who was behind the camera the day this was taken. Archie said he found it tucked under the boy's mattress after he died. He framed the photo and kept it where he could see it."

Declan nodded. "And the teddy bear?"

"Well, who could leave that sweet little thing alone in that cold, dark house? I mean, really? It didn't seem right."

Declan looked at both objects — the photo and the teddy bear. He remembered the first had been in Archie's room. The second, in Freddy's.

The bear had been sitting on the bed propped up on the pillows. It had a necklace of shiny plastic beads strung together on an elastic cord. Dangling from it was a little silver plastic heart with a heart-shaped paper sticker on it. There had been something written in pencil on the heart but it had been worn down to a ghostly shadow.

Katherine stared at the teddy bear fondly. "Funny thing with fathers and sons... When Freddy was alive, they never got along, and I never saw Archie say 'I love you' to the boy. But after Freddy died, Archie regretted that he hadn't made an effort to get along better and tell Freddy how he felt. Men are so stubborn!"

"Would you mind if I borrowed these?" he asked. "I just want to show them to my partner and see if he has any thoughts."

Katherine looked at the photo and the bear, then up at Declan. "You promise to bring them back as soon as you can?"

Declan gave a gentle smile. "I promise."

He left Katherine's house and carefully placed the photograph and the teddy bear in the cardboard box behind his seat. He'd show them to Charlie later and see if he had any ideas as to why Archie would have kept them for all these years.

Chapter Twenty

Charlie had been sitting at his desk for hours. He'd run internet image searches on the aged-up photos of Milo and so far he'd come up with nothing useful, unless Milo was a plumber in Iceland or a real estate agent in California. Neither was the right age, but they did share similar facial characteristics.

"Where are you, Milo?" he asked his computer.

Charlie looked at the search results and his gaze settled on the real estate agent from California. Milo's mother had moved back to California, maybe there was a link. Charlie pulled up his notes from Simon.

"Okay, time to move on. Michelle Coleman — let's see what we can find out about you."

The contact information that Simon had given Charlie was of no use. The phone number was disconnected and the address was now registered to a Tyrone Jennings.

The results of an internet search on 'Michelle Coleman movie star' came up quickly, though.

Michelle Hoffman, former glamour queen and starlet turned environmental activist, shares her trailer home with her two dogs, Dizzy and Bubs. They live in the off-grid "settlement" of Slab City, three hours east of San Diego in the Salton Trough area of the Sonoran Desert. The one-time up-and-coming movie actress, known as Michelle Coleman, was featured in such films as The Mountain *and the ill-fated remake of* Bus Stop *in which she recreated the role of Chérie, made famous by Marilyn Monroe. After the breakup of her third marriage with writer Mark Hoffman, she found her purpose in life – the promotion of a sustainable lifestyle.*

That was definitely her. Charlie decided to send an email to the writer of the internet piece and see if he had any way of getting in touch with Michelle.

Charlie went back to the image of the real estate agent, Mark Tupper. If Milo had escaped to California with his mother's help, could he have changed his name? Tupper had a large social media presence with accounts on Instagram, X, Threads and Facebook, but there was no mention of familial relations. His accounts were strictly for business.

Charlie looked at the mess of loose threads. He stood and wandered over to Mrs B's desk.

She looked up at him, staring over the top of her glasses. "Yes? May I help you?"

Charlie cocked his head. "Need any help?"

"No," she answered.

"Coffee?"

"Don't you have a crime to solve?" she asked.

"To be honest, I'm not having much luck."

She shrugged. "Sometimes you have to use the three Ps of good detective work."

Charlie frowned. *I don't remember them covering that in my PI course.* "What are they, Mrs B?"

"Patience, politeness and perseverance…and a bit of dumb luck doesn't hurt, either. I've got filing to do, so…"

Mrs B stared at him for a moment. "Go," she said as she pointed back to his desk.

Charlie went back to his computer and was surprised to discover that the writer of the article had already emailed back.

So, you're interested in Michelle Hoffman? Now why would a private investigator from Canada be wanting to interview that kook? Too many possibilities are rolling around in my head at the thought. She has no internet or phone. She thinks that having a cell phone is "giving into the corporate MAN" so you'll have to contact her by mail care of the general post office.

Good luck. You're going to need it.

Charlie sighed. This was going nowhere. It might be easier to send a message to Mark Tupper, the potential candidate for Simon's Milo. Charlie opted for the plain simple truth with this one.

I am acting on behalf of Simon Griffin of Banff, Alberta, Canada, former husband of Michelle Coleman Hoffman. He is trying to locate his long-lost son. Contact me if you have any information.

After typing the message, Charlie reread it. The only thing missing was something identifying Charlie as an African prince with a hefty inheritance that he wanted to share.

He considered what Mrs B had said then added the word 'please' to the final sentence. After all, it never hurt to be polite.

Charlie pressed 'send', then announced "I'm going out, Mrs B. It's time to utilise the fourth "P" of good detective work."

Mrs B frowned. "And that is?"

Charlie smiled. "Pastries," he said, then headed down the stairs.

When he got to Gwen's café, he opened the door a little too hard. She looked up quickly.

"Sorry," Charlie said.

He plunked himself down at a window seat and stared out into space.

Charlie heard the familiar sound of the espresso machine and milk steamer, then the glass door of the pastry cabinet sliding open and closed.

Gwen placed a latte and *pain au chocolat* in front of him, walked away then returned with her mug, taking the seat across from him. "What's Declan done this time?"

"Nothing. I mean he's done tons of things, but nothing wrong. He treats me like gold. He's been really supportive of me getting my PI licence."

"So what's wrong?" Gwen asked.

"Me—that's the problem. I feel like sometimes I don't know what the hell I'm doing."

"I suppose that's true of all of us," she said.

"Yeah, but usually I'm really good at computer stuff, and I can talk to people—they seem to like me. But this missing person case—I'm stumped. I've run out of things to look for online and I'm not sure who else to talk to. The kid I'm tracking has been gone for ten years, and the only person I've found who might be him, isn't him…unless he's had plastic surgery, but I think that really only happens in the movies."

"So have you been to the scene of the crime?" she asked.

"I don't think there'll be many clues lying around after a decade."

"Still, have you been out to the place where he was last seen?" Gwen persisted.

"Well, no," he answered sheepishly.

"And the missing guy, did he live by himself?"

"Well, he lived with his dad, and it's his father that's trying to find him. There's also a housekeeper that answers the phone…"

Gwen nodded her head. "You know, I've watched tons of detective shows on TV and I've learned a few things — housekeepers see and hear everything because their bosses don't remember that they're people too. They've become just part of the furniture. Okay, I've learned another thing — never watch murder mysteries with a cop. They just don't shut up about all the inaccuracies."

Charlie grinned. "Gwen, you're a genius!"

He knocked back his latte, trying to stifle a scream as it scalded his throat, then picked up the pastry, gave Gwen a quick hug and ran out of the café.

Charlie bounded up the stairs to his desk and called Simon's number.

"Griffin residence. How may I help you?"

"Yes, is Mr Griffin available? It's Charlie Watts from Declan Hunt Investigations calling."

"I'm sorry, Mr Watts, but Mr Griffin is unavailable at the moment. Shall I give him a message?"

"Am I speaking with Jasmine?"

"Yes."

"Mr Griffin told me about you. I was actually hoping I could ask you a few questions, if you have time."

"Well, I'm not sure if I —"

"I've been hired by Mr Griffin to investigate the disappearance of his son, Milo, ten years ago. I've already interviewed Mr Griffin, but if I could talk to you it would definitely help."

A voice in Charlie's head said, *Did you visit the scene of the crime?*

"Oh, and I was wondering if I could talk to you in person. Would tomorrow at one p.m. work for you?"

There was a pause at the other end of the line. "Mr Griffin did mention you. I don't suppose it would be a problem, but Mr Griffin has a business appointment tomorrow, so he won't be here."

"That's all right. Actually it's you I'm interested in talking to you, if you don't mind."

"Well, I suppose that would be fine."

"I'll see you then."

Let's see if the TV murder mysteries are right.

Chapter Twenty-One

Charlie's phone chirped with a text from Declan.

Leaving Katherine's. Meet me at Bar-None at five for a debrief?

Charlie replied.

See you then.

Charlie prepared some quick notes, then headed out of the office, waving to Mrs B. "I'll see you tomorrow. And don't forget to set the alarm."

"If someone would show me how, I'd be glad to do it, but…"

Charlie looked at the time. "Oh, right. I gotta run. I'll show you tomorrow."

He arrived at Bar-None at a quarter to five and found Mickey working behind the bar. In spite of the cold weather, he was dressed in a form-fitting black tank top. He'd dyed his hair icy-blue with white highlights. He looked like a very sexy Smurf.

"You're in early," Charlie said.

"Yeah. My daytime guy couldn't make it in, so I'm working both shifts today."

"Is it the flu?" Charlie asked.

"Not unless the flu is a muscular redhead named George. Now, what can I get you?"

"I'll take a…Alley Kat Pale Ale," he said after scoping out what was on the beer menu posted on the wall.

"Excellent choice. So, are you here alone or is the other half of the dynamic duo joining you?"

Charlie was about to reply when Declan walked in, planted a kiss on his lips and said, "I'll have what he's having."

They made their way over to Declan's favourite table in the back. After taking a sip of his drink, Declan asked, "How'd the day go?"

"Well, I had no luck finding the reclusive Michelle Coleman. She's only reachable by snail-mail unless we want to take a twenty-four-hour drive south. I had an iffy image match with the aged picture of Milo. It's a guy in the States who's probably too old—or it might just be the effects of too much time in the California sun. Anyway, I'm waiting to see if he gets back to me. On the positive side, thanks to a bit of inspiration from Gwen, I have an appointment to interview Simon's housekeeper Jasmine tomorrow afternoon. I'm hoping I can get her to dish the dirt on what happens in the Griffin household."

"That's all good news," Declan said. "At least you've got balls in the air. I had less success. Katherine didn't recognise any of the pictures of Milo you provided, so that's a bust. I did find out something interesting, however. It turns out that she's the executor of Archie's will."

"What?" Charlie said. "That gives her motive. As the executor, she can claim a percentage of the estate's value. And as the next-door neighbour, she's got plenty of opportunity."

"Slow down, Sherlock," Declan said. "Life's not always like it is on TV. But there was something else strange. She took a few things out of Archie's house. One was a stuffed bear that belonged to Freddy, and the other was a picture of Freddy that Archie had on his bedside table. She said they were special to Archie."

Declan took a long sip of his drink. "It doesn't make sense. What is it with fathers? I mean, there's Archie who basically set up a shrine for the kid he had no time for when he was alive. And then there's The Sarge and me…'adversarial' only begins to describe our relationship. I don't think he's ever once said that he loved me."

Charlie shrugged. "Maybe it's a guy thing. Maybe we've had it programmed into us that saying 'I love you' is a sign of weakness and we should never talk about it. I don't think I've ever said 'I love you' to my dad."

Charlie took a swig of his beer. "But I want that to change. And sooner than later. I'm tired of hiding my feelings."

Declan furrowed his brow. "Do I do that? With you, I mean? I hope not, because I'm not afraid to say that I love you."

Charlie leaned over and kissed him hard on the lips. "I love you, too."

Declan smiled. "So — work–life balance. How do you feel it's coming along?"

"Well...you were pulled away to deal with Katherine and I was gone to deal with Gran, so we're pretty well even there. I figure as long as we're communicating, we can make this work. And I *do* love working with you."

Declan gave Charlie a crooked grin. "Me too. Hey, I've got something I'd like you to give me a hand with, back at the office." Declan took Charlie's hand and slid it up toward his crotch. "If you're up for it?"

"Oh, I sure am."

They paid the tab and ran back to the apartment above the office. Charlie roughly pulled Declan's shirt off over his head as Declan frantically undid Charlie's belt while kicking off his own shoes. Charlie slid Declan's pants down to his ankles, then shoved him back on the bed, hauling his pants off, sending them flying across the room.

"Ooh, you bad boy," Charlie said. Declan was wearing no underwear. Charlie dove face first into Declan's crotch and started to nibble, lick and taste. He wrapped his hand around Declan's shaft and began fist pumping as he played with the tip of Declan's cock with his tongue and lips. Charlie was ravenous.

Declan moaned and said, "Slow down, Charlie. Slow down," but it was too late. Declan came. "Sorry. I was just so turned on. God, I've missed you."

Charlie grinned. "Oh, not to worry. We've got all night. We're just getting started. Give me a second. I just have to go to the bathroom."

Charlie went to the cabinet below the sink to get some supplies for a night of fun.

When he came back, Declan was on the phone.

"Gary... I don't think it's anything to worry about... Tomorrow. Morning... All right. See you then."

Declan disconnected. He had a frown on his face.

"Is there a problem?" Charlie asked.

Declan put his phone on the nightstand. "It seems the cops were keeping an eye on Archie's place after all. They saw me at Katherine O'Grady's and wanted to know what I've been up to. I've been summoned to the office to explain myself."

"Are you in any trouble?" Charlie asked.

"I'll find out tomorrow. In the meantime, I think we should finish what we started just in case I can't use my 'Get Out Of Jail' card."

* * * *

Charlie tossed and turned in bed. He got up to go to the bathroom, but something was wrong. He looked over and Declan was sound asleep, snoring softly. The only light in the room came from the alarm clock on Declan's side table. The clock read three a.m. Charlie scanned the room. He sensed he was being watched. If something was about to go down, Charlie had to be sure it wasn't just his imagination.

There was definitely movement in the shadows beside the bathroom door. Someone stepped into view. It was Dave, the burnt barista from Charlie's dream the other night. The ghost sipped at his coffee, and as he stared at Charlie, something began to happen. A delicate shimmer surrounded Dave, then he began to shrink. Whatever was happening, it didn't seem to concern him. He just stood, stared, sipped and shrank...and altered form. As his height diminished, his proportions changed. His skin was no longer blackened and tattered. Dave was changing into a young boy. *Was this what he looked like as a kid?* Charlie wondered.

Dave was also dressed differently. He wore a little sailor suit complete with cap. His skin had reverted to the fresh pink of a healthy young child. And Dave now had hair! It was long, curly and blond. The young Dave smiled at Charlie and winked, then ran into the shadows calling out, "Bye, Baby Bunting. Daddy's gone a-hunting, to get a little rabbit-skin, to hide his Baby Bunting in. *Find me!*"

Charlie tried to scream, but nothing came out. The next thing he knew, he was sitting up in bed gasping for air. Declan was still asleep beside him. He'd been dreaming, but it had felt so real. Charlie snuggled back into Declan and tried to sleep, but he kept seeing movement in the shadows wherever he looked. Charlie could feel the ghosts in the building, and for some reason, they were trying to tell him something.

Chapter Twenty-Two

Declan stood at the front desk of the police station. The cop on duty didn't even look up. "Take a seat."

Declan turned around and sat in one of the available chairs. Across from him there was a young mother with a baby on her lap, a toddler on one side and a smelly old man on the other. Declan glanced at the baby, who beamed a brilliant, toothless smile at him. He couldn't help but smile back.

"Oh no, you didn't," the mother said, picking up the baby and sniffing its diaper. "Of all the times to…"

She glanced at Declan. "I know the washroom's too tight for me and both kids. I'll only be a minute. Would you mind?" She nodded toward the toddler, then headed off to the washroom with the baby and a large diaper bag. As the washroom door was closing, she poked her head back out and hollered, "Her name is Susie!"

Susie stared up at him and smiled. Declan stuck his thumbs in his ears, waggled his fingers and made a silly face. The smile on Susie's face instantly disappeared and turned into a pout that was far too large for such a little head. Then she began to cry. No, not cry…wail.

Declan instinctively picked her up and stared into her eyes. "Shh, shh, you're okay. You're okay."

The cop at the desk lifted his head. "Could you please do something about your child?"

"She's not mine," Declan responded. This might have been the wrong thing to say.

Another cop showed up on the scene. "If you can't control your child, I'm going to have to ask you to leave."

"He says it's not his," said the cop at the desk.

"Then whose is it?"

"The mother just up and left," the smelly man said.

The second cop looked carefully at Declan. "Hey— aren't you—"

The baby was now in full 'scream' mode.

"What the hell's going on out there?" a voice shouted. It was Gary Sawchuck.

"Declan?" Sawchuck said, taking the toddler away from him and raising her up in his arms. She began to calm down.

"Uh, her name is Susie," Declan offered.

"Professor Diller?" the second cop called out. "If you'll come with me, please."

The smelly guy stood and followed the cop, but not before he turned to Declan and said, "You'll make a terrible father."

Declan was relieved when the bathroom door opened and Susie's mother returned.

"You have a beautiful daughter," Sawchuck said, handing Susie back to her.

"Thank you—hey, has anyone seen my father? He was just there." She pointed to the now empty chair across from Declan.

"The professor?" Declan asked.

"Yes!"

"They just came to collect him. They went that-a-way," he said, pointing down the nearest hall.

"Oh, Jesus." She slung the baby bag over her neck and took a child in each arm, then ran down the hall. "Dad, don't say anything until the lawyer shows up!"

Sawchuck shook his head. "See. Things haven't changed much since you left, have they? Come on. Let's go to my office where we can talk in private."

Declan walked through a tightly packed series of desks. He vaguely recognised a few of the officers.

"What's he doing back?" one said.

"In for questioning, probably," the other replied.

Then he heard it — "Fag."

Declan turned around and caught the eye of the officer who had whispered the last word. "You should know."

The guy leapt to his feet but Sawchuck intervened. "At least *try* to behave like adults!"

Declan followed Sawchuck to his office and took a seat. "Like I said — some things never change." He moved behind his desk and sat down. "Let's get down to business. I wanted to check in with you on the investigation of Archie Whitcher's murder. As I told you last night, we've had the house under surveillance."

"Oh?" Declan replied.

"Yeah. That neighbour of his has been coming and going from Archie's house on a regular basis."

"And you didn't try and stop her?" Declan asked.

Sawchuck paused. "We were more interested in watching from a distance to see what she was up to. Got any ideas?"

"Well, I can tell you, she's got a key. She said she was going over to make sure the heat was on so the pipes wouldn't freeze."

Sawchuck leaned forward. "How very neighbourly of her. And of you, too."

"What do you mean?"

"Well, other than that first time you said you went into Archie's house, you've been there two other times since we started surveillance."

"Not to Archie's house, I haven't," Declan deflected.

"No. You were visiting Kathrine O'Grady. You seem to be getting kinda chummy with her."

"I'm just trying to clarify information that may help with my enquiries. She phoned me because she was scared. She said she thought she saw the man in the brown coat come back and it made her nervous. Have you had any luck tracking him down?"

Sawchuck frowned. "Not enough to go on. You say he came back?"

"Yeah."

Sawchuck picked up a folder and flipped through some pages. "I've had no report of anyone matching that description calling on her. Are you sure about that?"

"That's what she said. Maybe your watchdog took a nap."

"Hmm. I'll look into it. What else can you tell me about her?" Sawchuck asked.

"She knows how to handle a gun. She pointed one at me when we first met."

"Oh?"

Declan cocked his head. "What kind of gun did you say Archie was shot with?"

"I didn't. But it was a nine-millimetre handgun. Why?"

"Katherine's is a shotgun."

Sawchuck nodded. "Okay, I'll make a note of it. Anything else?"

"You might find it interesting that she's the executor of Archie's will."

Sawchuck looked up from the file. "Now that is interesting."

"And she doesn't know a Milo that was associated with either Freddy or Archie," Declan added.

"She told you all of this?"

"Uh-huh."

"Why didn't you tell us sooner?" Sawchuck asked.

"I only found out yesterday."

Sawchuck stared at Declan. "Anything else?"

Declan considered telling him about the licence number of the car that she had photographed, but he decided to hold onto that for the time being until he knew if it was important or not. "That's it."

Gary sighed. "So, you have a woman who is familiar with firearms, denies all knowledge of who might have wanted to kill her shady neighbour, sees mysterious men lurking about that none of our officers have seen *and* who is the executor of the deceased's estate... Do you think it might just be possible that she's lying to you? Because to me — and let's ignore all of my years of policing — to me she's starting to look like a prime suspect."

"Do you really think she could have done it?"

Sawchuck looked intently at Declan, "I don't think she'd have the physical strength to inflict the beating Archie took before he was shot. And she had no gunpowder residue on her hands...and yes, we tested. But that doesn't mean she isn't involved. So I just want to be clear, that if you have any other insights, you should share them with us. Got it?"

Declan nodded.

"Now, get out of here before you get us both into trouble."

Declan rose from his seat and headed to his van. If Sawchuck's men were telling the truth, it was possible that Katherine O'Grady was playing Declan for a fool. But why?

Chapter Twenty-Three

Charlie enjoyed his drive out to Banff in The Beast. It had been a long time since he'd taken the muscle car out on the highway and felt the power of its engine. He pulled up to the intercom in front of Simon's property and pressed the button. Within moments, the big steel gate slowly swung open.

As Charlie parked in front of the house, the door opened. A tall woman, who appeared to be in her mid-fifties, poked her nose out. "Mr Watts, I presume?"

"Yes. Is it okay if I park here?" Charlie asked.

"That will be just fine."

Charlie made his way into the house and removed his coat. The *Rocky Mountain Leisure* magazine was right—The Paddock was magnificent.

Charlie's thoughts were interrupted when Jasmine said, "I hope that old car of yours has a good heater."

"That car has a better heater than my apartment."

She looked out of the window at The Beast. "I love to see a beautiful car like that. So many of the ones you see around these days all look the same. They have no style. Not like yours. Now, come with me into the kitchen. Do you prefer tea or coffee?"

"I love both. I'll have whatever you're having."

Charlie sat in the sunlit room, admiring the panoramic view of the mountains through the bay window as the woman prepared a pot of tea.

"Sorry, I haven't properly introduced myself—I'm Jasmine Robertson, but you can call me Jasmine."

"And you can call me Charlie. I never was a Charles. My family has a tradition of always going straight for the nickname."

"Just cut to the chase. I like that."

She set a plate of Nanaimo bars on the table. "Help yourself. I'll bet a young man like yourself loves sweets, and I bet you never put on a pound. Trust me—that won't last forever." She laughed.

Charlie was immediately taken with her.

She poured the tea and let Charlie help himself to milk and sugar. She took hers strong and black.

"So," she started, "you want to know about young Milo?"

"Yes. Do you mind if I take a few notes?"

"No, go right ahead."

Charlie opened his note pad. "I'm just trying to get the fullest picture of him that I can. What kind of boy was he?"

Jasmine settled back into her chair. Charlie could sense that she was looking through a decade of life to get back to the time when Milo was living in this house.

"He was a good boy. A kind boy. I'll never forget that he always remembered my birthday."

"Did he have many friends?" Charlie asked.

"No. He was usually on his own. He was always reading and he liked to spend a lot of time outdoors, even in the winter. He loved looking for animals and taking their pictures. Milo also had a particular fascination with history. I think he got that from his father. Mr Griffin lives and breathes history. I remember him saying to Milo once, 'Boy, you were born to be part of ancient history.'"

"So Milo got along with his father?"

"Not exactly. Milo and Mr Griffin weren't on friendly terms. It was definitely a father-son relationship where Mr Griffin insisted he be shown respect — as he should have. I think one of the reasons Milo didn't have a lot of friends was that Mr Griffin was really protective of the boy. What you'd expect from a man with...well, let's just say he's not hurting for money."

"Do you think he was concerned that someone might take advantage of Milo?"

She nodded. "When you are rich, you've got to think of those things."

"When Milo disappeared, did Mr Griffin ever think that the boy might have been kidnapped?"

"At first he did, but no one ever asked for a ransom — at least not that I heard of. The police just thought the boy got it in his mind to run away and live his own life."

Jasmine took a long sip of her tea. "I never felt that Milo was happy here. I think he may have felt a bit like a prisoner. Even when he was old enough to go for walks on his own, he had to take one of us with him."

"One of you had to go with him?"

"Oh, yes." She smiled. "Sometimes me. Sometimes one of the others. He was never supposed to be without us except when he was on the property, or in class at school."

"So there are more staff than just you?"

"There used to be. We used to have a full-time gardener and a maintenance man. Now we just hire as needed. We still have Mr Semple."

Charlie leaned in. "And what does Mr Semple do?"

"Well, he's Mr Griffin's right-hand man. He's been with him for even longer than I have."

"Does he live here?" Charlie asked.

"Not full-time, but he does have a bedroom upstairs for times when Mr Griffin wants him here. In the early days, he was usually the one who kept his eye on Milo."

Charlie looked up from his note pad. "Sort of a personal bodyguard then?"

"You could say that."

"And this Mr Semple, could I have his first name? Just for the records. My boss is a real stickler for the details, if you know what I mean."

"Oh, I understand that," she said. "It's Tom."

"Is he in today?"

"Not at the moment, but he might be here later this evening when Mr Griffin gets back."

"So, getting back to Milo," Charlie said, "you mentioned he was rarely on his own off the property other than at school?"

"Well…he'd still manage to sneak away from time to time. He was a boy, after all. Always dreaming of adventure, and he was tired of waiting to grow up."

Charlie reviewed his notes. "Mr Griffin told me they had a fight the night he ran away."

She sighed. "Boys and their fathers always fight, don't they?"

Yup, Charlie thought.

"And usually about the simplest things," she added.

"Do you have any idea what they fought about that night?" Charlie asked.

"I do remember something about Milo being in the vault in his father's office, and some money. Later on, Mr Griffin said five thousand dollars was missing. It didn't make sense. Why would a boy who had everything want to steal?"

To get away from this prison...

Charlie made a note. "And Mr Griffin said that Milo had a...special friend?"

She stared off into the distance. "Yes, but Milo was very secretive about it."

"Did you ever meet him, or did Milo ever mention his name?"

"No, I never met him and, no, he never mentioned a name."

"Thank you. Just one more question. Have you seen this?" Charlie passed her the copy of the note that was supposedly from Milo. "Mr Griffin said it arrived last week."

She glanced at it. "I never saw what it said, but I'm guessing it's the one that was brought to the door."

Charlie's eyes widened. "You mean it didn't come in the mail?"

"No. It was delivered by a boy."

"A boy? How old?"

Her eyes narrowed. "Fifteen. Maybe a bit younger."

Charlie had an idea. He looked at his watch. They had time.

"Would you recognise him again if you saw him?"

"Possibly," she said, nodding.

"Would you be willing to try and identify him? Now, I mean. School will be getting out soon, and I don't know when I'll next be getting back to Banff. It could be a clue that'll help me find out what happened to Milo."

It's a long shot, but why not?

Jasmine smiled. "I can see why Mr Griffin hired you. Let's go get our coats and maybe you can give me a ride in that car of yours."

Chapter Twenty-Four

Simon was uneasy when Jasmine told him that Charlie was coming out to interview her while he was away, but Simon knew she could be trusted not to reveal any of the secrets of Monarch Holdings — secrets that had been weighing on his mind a great deal lately. He'd decided that today's business couldn't wait any longer, just in case Harlen Feist rallied from his latest malady.

It took him almost two hours to get to his destination. A long line of cars had slowed to see a small herd of elk at the side of the road near the park boundary. Some people had even gotten out of their cars to get a selfie with the animals. Simon had sat in the traffic jam wishing the elk would gore one of them just to teach them a lesson. Their stupidity had added an extra twenty minutes to his journey.

It was a little after two when Simon finally pulled his rental Audi A6 into the parking lot of Calgary's Tom Baker Cancer Centre. The car was the best the insurance company could give him while his beloved Bentley was being repaired. It felt like riding in a four-wheel insult. He was careful not to get road salt on Tom's camelhair coat when he stepped out of the car. Simon wasn't the only one who was precious about his belongings. He wrapped a scarf up around his face, and donned a pair of aviator sunglasses. He cursed as a gust of wind almost blew the fedora off his head. Simon normally bundled up in more practical clothing, but he wanted to make sure that if any of the staff was asked to identify him later, that the person they described would be dressed in Tom's clothing.

Simon walked into the hospital and encountered a pretty young woman at the visitor information desk.

"Good day, sir. May I help you?"

"Yes… I'm here to see Harlen Feist. He's having treatments of some sort and I was told that he was here. I assume he's still, uh, 'up-and-running'."

"Up-and-running?" she asked.

"You know…heart still beating and all that."

"Oh… Let me see."

She plugged away at the computer for a moment. "Yes. Your friend is, as you say, up-and-running. Let me give you a map to show you where you can find him."

She highlighted a route on a floor plan of the hospital and passed it to him.

"Thank you, my dear," he said, then headed off to find Harlen.

When he finally managed to navigate the maze of hallways, he was surprised to discover that Harlen was in a semi-private room. *He couldn't afford private?* As Simon walked through the door, he noted the other bed was currently vacant. *Thank God.*

Simon looked at the once-mighty Harlen Feist lying in bed, hooked up to countless machines. The disease had aged him. He wasn't the fit seventy-year-old that Simon had remembered. His eyes were closed, but the heart monitor showed he still had a pulse.

Simon sat himself in the chair beside the bed. The journey into town had worn him out, and he shut his eyes preparing himself for the job ahead.

"How long have you been here?" a voice said, startling him.

"Not long. So... Nature's given you a bit of a kick, has it, Harlen?"

"More than a kick. More like a full-body check into the boards."

Simon nodded. He found these situations awkward. He was never sure what to say. "So, are they treating you well here?"

"Pretty good. At least the nurses are pretty to look at," Feist said with a laugh that turned into a body-wracking cough.

Simon waited until Feist's cough had calmed down, then asked, "Do you have everything in order?"

"Just about."

"Good. It's always good to tie up the loose ends while you can."

"Is that why you're here, Simon? Looking for a bit of a nod of approval from the old man?"

"Actually, I just hate to think of people alone in hospitals."

Harlen scowled. "Yeah. Right. The old man is down and the buzzards are circling, hoping to pick at the carcass."

"Now, Harlen. No need to be so negative. You need a healthy state of mind if you're ever going to beat this."

"I'm not going to beat this," Harlen said, "and we both know it." He broke out into another coughing fit, then he continued. "So I suspect you think you're taking over Monarch Holdings?"

Simon nodded. "I've earned it. I just wanted to hear you say it before you die."

Harlen coughed again. "You were my first choice, but recently I've had some disturbing information that suggests that you may have had something to do with my son Roger's death. So, needless to say, I've changed my mind. I don't think I can trust you anymore, Simon. In fact, my lawyer is on his way over right now with the paperwork to name my new successor. You can sign as a witness."

Simon took off his glasses and smiled. "Well, it looks like I got here just in time, then."

* * * *

Simon walked down the hall, heading toward the hospital exit. He walked with a bounce in his step, feeling like life had just gotten better.

Several nurses ran past him. One yelled out to the other, "Crash cart's on its way."

He knew they'd be heading to Harlen Feist's room. He also knew that there wasn't a crash cart built that could revive him now.

Chapter Twenty-Five

When Charlie and Jasmine arrived at the Banff Community High School, the students were just getting out.

"What do you remember about the boy that delivered the note?" Charlie asked.

"He was shorter than you," she said, "and he was wearing a toque. Strange, though, he was wearing a Montreal Canadiens jacket. Everyone from around here supports either the Calgary Flames or the Edmonton Oilers. A boy supporting the Montreal hockey team would not last long here."

"So, you think he could be from out east?"

"Not necessarily. His coat was old and patched. It might have been all he could get from the thrift shop."

It didn't take long for the schoolyard to clear. The kids that remained took turns hurling snowballs and insults at a crudely constructed snowman that they called Mr Wright. Charlie wondered what course he taught.

Just as Charlie was ready to admit that this had been futile, Jasmine tapped his shoulder.

"That's it. That's the coat," she said, indicating the lone boy who was leaving the school. "He must have had a detention."

"Okay, you stay in the car. I'll be back."

Charlie jumped out and started to follow the boy.

After a few blocks, when they were out of view of anyone at the school and on a small side street that led to Banff Avenue, Charlie called out, "Hey kid."

The boy looked over his shoulder. "Get the fuck away from me, perv," he called back and kept walking.

"I'm not a perv. I'm a private investigator," Charlie shouted out.

The boy stopped, turned and faced him. "Private investigators can't be pervs?"

"You've got me there, kid. I just want some information," Charlie said.

The boy turned and walked away.

"And I'm willing to pay for it," Charlie added.

"So you *are* a perv."

"Like I said, I'm just looking for some information, that's all. I understand someone had you deliver a letter last week to the big house on Buffalo Street. I'm trying to find out who it was."

The boy stopped and looked around. He was obviously either trying to figure out if anyone else was listening, or scoping out a place to run.

Declan had told Charlie that whenever he went into the field, he should always carry cash with him, because he never knew when a bribe would be necessary…and no one would accept credit. Declan had also said it should be at least a few hundred dollars. That way if he got mugged, the attacker would be less likely to kill him, especially if they felt their effort in robbing him had been adequately rewarded.

"A hundred bucks," Charlie offered. It would be Griffin's money, so he didn't care. He could go higher if he had to.

The boy cocked his head like a dog processing a command. "A hundred bucks and I just have to give you information?"

"Yup."

The boy chewed on his lip. "Must have been something important in that letter to be worth a hundred bucks."

"Yup. And something you don't want to be involved in. You give me the info, I give you the money and we'll never see each other again, okay? Pretty simple."

This is going well.

"A hundred and fifty," the boy said.

What? This kid was a pro.

The boy added, "One-fifty or I start screaming that you touched me."

"One-fifty it is. And no screaming."

The boy nodded and walked a few feet closer. "So here's what happened. This guy, probably in his twenties, came up to me in the arcade and offered me money to deliver a letter. That's it."

"That's it? I pretty well could'a figured that much out on my own."

"Then pay yourself a hundred and fifty."

Charlie wasn't going to give up. "Describe him."

"Okay. He was about your height, maybe a little shorter. He was white. No accent."

Charlie pulled out his phone and showed the boy the aged photograph of Milo. "Could this have been him?"

The boy glanced at it and shrugged.

"Have a *good* look at it," Charlie said.

The boy stared longer at the image. "Nope. The guy I saw had long dark hair. Kinda looked like a hippie."

Not much to go on there.

"What else can you tell me? What was he dressed like?"

"A parka. Had a few taped patches. He wore jeans and Kodiak boots. Real stylish." He laughed. The boy was starting to relax.

Charlie nodded. "Did he ever mention his name?"

"Not that I can remember."

"Anything else about that afternoon? Did he have a car?"

The boy shook his head. "Not that I saw. But there *was* one other thing. He did seem to know the place."

"The place on Buffalo Street?"

"Yeah. He knew just how to sneak around the iron fence. There's a big cedar bush beside a stone pillar. If you push back the branches, there's a gap you can get through. And he knew that the place had a lady that answered the door for the owner."

Charlie nodded. "He did, did he?"

"Yeah," the boy confirmed.

"Anything else?"

"Nope. Money, please." The boy held out his hand.

Charlie pulled out his wallet and counted out eight twenties. "Guess you wouldn't have change?"

"Do I look like a bank teller?"

Charlie handed him the money. The boy shoved the bills into his jeans pocket, turned then walked away trailing a stream of exhaled steam. He was a con artist in the making. Charlie admired him.

* * * *

Charlie drove Jasmine back to The Paddock. When he got there, the gate was open and there was a black BMW 7 Series sedan parked in the drive.

"When is that man going to learn to shut the gate?" Jasmine complained.

Charlie looked over at her.

"You don't know this town, Mr Watts. You leave that gate open and in no time the property's full of tourists taking pictures like this is a public garden."

"Is that Mr Griffin's car?" Charlie asked.

"No. It's too modern for him. That's Mr Semple's."

"The guy that works for Mr Griffin?"

"That's him," she replied. "Mr Griffin calls him his 'major-domo', a title Tom's very good at using when he's staying here. Would you like to speak with him?"

"If he has the time," Charlie answered.

"Why don't you park on the street?" Jasmine said. "If Mr Griffin returns and there's not a parking space for his car in the drive, the angels in heaven will have to cover their ears."

Charlie smiled. "Just gimme a sec, if you don't mind. Could you leave the gate open for a few more minutes until I get in?"

"I'll wait for you here."

Charlie parked down the street. Before he returned to the gate, he followed the fence line to a dense, two-metre-high cedar which grew beside a large stone pillar. He pushed the shrub away from the brickwork. There it was—the gap the boy had told him about. When he returned to the gate, Jasmine had a look of concern on her face.

"You may want to fill in that gap over there," he said. "Makes it pretty easy for people to break in."

As they passed through the gates, Jasmine searched through her purse and retrieved her key ring. She pressed a button on a fob and the gates quietly closed behind them.

They walked up to the house and through the front door. Charlie could hear a voice from another room. The person speaking sounded like they were in the midst of a heated discussion. "I don't care how much it costs. Get it done."

A man walked into the foyer. He was taller than Charlie, and appeared to be in his mid to late fifties. His salt-and-pepper hair was well-coiffed and suited his handsome face — one that looked like it had seen a fair bit of physical action over the years. The man wore a well-tailored suit over his muscular frame. He could have been a boxer in his earlier years. When he spotted Charlie, his brow furrowed. "Who the hell is this?" he asked Jasmine.

Charlie extended his hand. "Charlie Watts. I work for Declan Hunt. You must be Mr Semple."

Semple took his hand with a controlled firm grip. Charlie suspected that he could crush his hand if he wanted to.

"Hunt? The detective?"

"That's right."

Semple nodded. "Ah, yes. I recognise you now. You're working for Simon, trying to find Milo."

"I am. I'm just in the initial phase of the investigation."

Semple crossed his arms. "I'm the one who referred Mr Hunt to Simon. I hope you won't make me look bad."

"I always try to avoid that," Charlie said. "Tell me, Mr Semple—"

"Tom. Why don't you come into the living room?"

He turned to Jasmine and said in a sharp tone, "By the way, my long camelhair coat was supposed to be back from the cleaners last night. Call and see if it's ready. And maybe when I'm done with Mr Watts, you can tell me what the two of you have been up to."

Jasmine disappeared into the kitchen and Tom led Charlie into the other room and sat down on a leather sofa. "So, how can I help you?"

"Well, Tom. You seem to be the kind of guy that has his finger on the pulse of the people here…"

Charlie hoped flattery would help grease the wheels. "I've been building up a dossier on Milo and I was hoping that you could help me fill in a few blanks."

"I'll do what I can."

Charlie continued. "I understand that aside from the RCMP, you also led an investigation for Mr Griffin when his son went missing ten years ago."

"I did. Neither of us got very far."

"Is it safe to assume that the boy's room was thoroughly searched after his disappearance?"

"I looked it over," Tom said.

"But not the police?"

"They did, after me."

And what did you find that wasn't there when the police searched? Charlie thought. "It's my understanding you help Mr Griffin with his business dealings? Is that correct?"

"I do."

"At the time of Milo's disappearance, do you remember any business enemies that would have wanted to use Milo as leverage?"

"No."

"And what exactly is Mr Griffin's business?" Charlie asked.

"Import-export." Tom's steel-blue eyes burnt into Charlie's.

"Import and export of what?"

"Things that need to be imported and exported. Simon Griffin is a…generalist."

Charlie smiled and nodded. It was clear that Tom Semple was trained not to answer.

"One other thing, Tom. Mr Griffin mentioned that Milo had a friend."

Tom's muscles tensed.

Bingo. What does he know, and who is he trying to protect?

Charlie pressed on. "Mr Griffin believed that Milo had made friends with another boy. Do you know who he was?"

"No."

"With all of your resources," Charlie persisted, "you never tracked down the boy Milo was seeing?"

"I don't think Milo saw this other boy often. I suspect it was the few times that he snuck away from school when I wasn't watching him. Milo was good at keeping secrets."

Charlie sensed he was lying. "One last thing. Do you remember the night that Milo disappeared?"

"That was ten years ago."

"Ten years this week," Charlie clarified. "Were you here at the house?"

Tom paused. "I was. As I recall, I told the police that after dinner I went to my quarters. I didn't like to hang around when Simon and Milo were having a fight."

"Do you remember what they were fighting about?"

"No. It was personal and had nothing to do with me," he said instantly.

"And Milo left later that evening?"

"Apparently so. Simon banged on my door to tell me his Bentley was gone."

"Gone? Like stolen? From the gated drive?"

Tom nodded. "We both knew that Milo had taken it."

"But he was fifteen," Charlie said. "He only would have had his learner's permit."

"He was probably a better driver at fifteen than his father ever was. Look—I trained him how to drive when he was thirteen. He needed to be able to protect himself. There was always the chance that someone might try to kidnap him to get control over Simon. I wanted him to have every advantage in a situation like that."

Charlie paused. "I guess that makes sense. So Milo borrowed his father's car. Where did he go?"

"I tracked the car to the airport," Tom replied. "Simon insisted on putting tracking devices in all of his vehicles as soon as the technology was available. I have no idea where Milo ended up. We checked all outgoing flights and his identification wasn't associated with any passenger."

"He just vanished?"

"He did...or someone else made him disappear."

Tom's phone rang. "I'm sorry, I have to take this. It's business." He got up from the couch and yelled out, "Jasmine, can you open the gate for Mr Watts so he can get back to Calgary?"

As Charlie made his way to the foyer, Tom went into another room and closed the door. Jasmine appeared.

She pressed a button on a panel by the front entrance and said, "I'll close the gate once you're through."

Charlie quickly headed back to The Beast and texted Declan.

Be back in a few hours. Found out a few interesting things. Tracked down the boy who delivered the note and one other thing, Simon's right-hand man has a camelhair coat. Possible connection to Katherine's mystery man?

Chapter Twenty-Six

Declan walked up the stairs to the office carrying a paper bag from Gwen's. Mrs B was still at her desk, tidying up before she left for the day.

"What are you doing here so late?" he asked.

"Avoiding getting home too early. My sister Irene has her weekly knitting circle at the apartment every Wednesday and if I have to put up with those old biddies again..."

"You do realise that you're probably older than some of those 'old biddies'."

She glowered at him. "You've obviously never experienced what needles and wool can do to a middle-aged woman. It's enough to make you want to choke them with their own yarn. Whinge, whine, complain..." she muttered as she packed her belongings in her bag and went off to get her coat.

"Here," he said, passing her the paper bag. "They're end-of-day pastries Gwen gave me. I think you could use them more than Charlie."

She pulled out a custard tart and devoured it. "You may have just prevented a homicide. I'll see you tomorrow, and thanks for this." She gently placed the pastry bag into her carryall and headed out through the door.

Declan went into his office and poured himself a drink. He sat, feet up on the desk, and sipped, enjoying the silence. At times it was good to be alone.

He thought back to his meeting with Gary Sawchuck. How could he have missed the surveillance vehicle on the street? Was he getting sloppy? And Katherine's man in the brown coat that no one else saw... If she was playing him, was there any way she could have killed Archie? Then there was Charlie's text... Too many coincidences, and Declan hated coincidences.

Declan's cell phone rang. He looked at the caller's number and picked it up. "Martin! Thanks for getting back to me."

"Hope I'm not catching you at a bad time."

"Not at all. I'm just sitting here enjoying a bit of peace and quiet."

Declan drained his glass, slid his feet off the desk and grabbed a pen and a piece of paper. "Now, any luck on the licence plate?"

"Was the car you were looking for a 2000 grey Chevy Impala?"

"That's it."

"It belongs to a Florence Keough on Geikie Street in Jasper. Here's her address."

Declan jotted down the details. "What else do you know about her?"

"Not much to tell from what I have here. She was born March 23, 1947. I can get you info on her insurer if that would be of any use?"

"No, don't worry about that, Martin. This is perfect for what I need. I really appreciate it."

"Appreciate it enough to meet me at The Greek sometime? You can bring that young male assistant of yours. He looks like he could be a lot of fun."

The thought of dragging Charlie off to The Greek for what Martin had in mind made Declan laugh out loud. He could only imagine the look on Charlie's face if he suggested it.

"Thanks for the invite, but we're trying to make a go of it on our own, if you know what I mean."

"So sad," Martin said. "Oh, well. I'll just have to keep reliving the memories, I guess. I'll say hello to Mateo and the boys at The Greek for you."

"You do that. Take good care of yourself, and thanks for the information."

Declan hung up and pondered what Martin had shared with him.

Now, what would a seventy-eight-year-old be doing driving down from Jasper to Calgary in winter?

Declan turned to his computer and did a reverse lookup on the address. Charlie wasn't the only one who could find people on the internet. And there she was.

He phoned the number and after a few rings, the call was answered.

"Hello?" a voice said.

"May I speak to Florence Keough?"

"Speaking." The voice sounded hesitant.

"Ms Keough, I'm sorry to disturb you—"

"If you're trying to sell me something, don't waste your breath. I've got everything I need. And if you're trying to save my soul, don't bother. I got rid of that years ago."

Declan liked this woman already.

"I'm doing neither, Ms Keough. I promise."

"And you can drop the whole 'Ms' business. I was married once and death didn't take that away from me."

"Mrs Keough it is, then," Declan said. "My name's Declan Hunt and I'm a private investigator from Calgary. I'm looking into an incident that happened in the Forest Lawn neighbourhood of Calgary last Thursday."

She hadn't hung up yet, so that was a good sign.

"What kind of incident?" she asked.

"I'm sorry to say it was a murder and a car matching your Impala was spotted on 43rd Street, SE. Were you in Calgary on Thursday?"

"A murder," she repeated.

Declan tried to read the tone of her voice. There was no inflection that expressed shock or surprise.

"And you think I was involved?" she accused.

"Nothing of the sort, Mrs Keough. I'm really just trying to determine why your car was there that day. You couldn't imagine the number of people that end up on lists like these during an investigation. That's why crimes take so long to solve. It's not like you see on television. I just need to find out if you were in Calgary on Thursday."

There was a brief silence before she responded. "You must be mistaken. I was away almost all week visiting my sister in Edmonton, so there is no way I could have been in Calgary."

"Are you sure? Because a car with your licence plate was seen on the street last Thursday."

"I'm not answering any more of your questions. I have to go."

She hung up.

Declan looked at the photo of the car on his phone. *Well, if it wasn't you, then someone had your car that day and I want to know who.*

Declan's thoughts were interrupted by a voice that called out. "I'm back!" Charlie poked his head in though Declan's door. "Just give me a sec to get out of my winter gear, then I'll give you a proper hello."

A moment later Charlie walked in, leaned over and gave Declan a deep kiss. Charlie smacked his lips. "Mmm, someone's had a scotch." He walked over to the credenza and poured himself a finger of the golden liquid.

"Yes, please," Declan said, holding up his glass.

"Yes, sir!" Charlie replied.

When Charlie had refilled his drink, Declan slid his hand up the back of Charlie's leg, stopping when he reached his rock-hard buttocks. He sighed and accepted the glass.

"Something tells me we're not going to be going out tonight," Charlie said.

"Not if I have anything to say about it. But first..." Declan raised his glass in a toast. "To your great Banff excursion. I've gotta say, your text intrigued me. So tell me what you found out."

Charlie plopped himself into a chair. "First of all, to call Jasmine a housekeeper seems a little...insufficient. It's a gut feeling, but I think there's more to her than meets the eye. Anyway, she helped me find the boy who delivered the note to Simon. The kid told me that the guy who had him drop it off was in his twenties and had long black hair — said he looked like a hippie."

"Did the kid get paid to do it?" Declan asked.

"I don't think that he would do anything for free. That kid's a wheeler-dealer in the making. I also met a guy named Tom Semple. He's a tough one. Looks like he spent a good deal of time fighting. And winning."

Declan jotted down the name. "What's his role in all of this?"

"He's supposedly Simon's right-hand man, and was a bodyguard for Milo."

"Now what would a kid like Milo need a bodyguard for, unless daddy was involved in something he shouldn't have been?"

"Jasmine said it was because of Simon's money. When I asked Semple to clarify what Simon did for a living, he was more than a little evasive. Come to think of it, he was not very forthcoming with the answers to any of the questions," Charlie added.

"I've known guys like that before."

Charlie continued, "So when I found out he had a camelhair coat, all of a sudden I remembered what Katherine had said to you. She said that the mystery man wore an expensive, long light-brown coat. And he looked like a stylish gangster."

Declan pondered this. He took another sip of scotch. "Could be a coincidence. Probably that's all it is. Those coats are pretty common…"

"Yeah. Probably just a coincidence."

They both sat in silence before Declan said, "I mean, what would connect a man like Tom Semple to a low-end bottom-feeder like Archie Whitcher?"

Charlie took a sip of his scotch. "Yeah. Archie was definitely a crook and Semple is working with Simon in import-export, whatever that really means."

Declan put down his glass on the desk. "Wait. Katherine said Archie used to store lots of boxes of stuff for other people in his basement."

"Lots of boxes?" Charlie asked.

"Truckloads, sometimes. Like they were maybe from…"

"An import-export business?"

Charlie leaned forward. "What if Archie had been skimming a little off the top? And what if this came to the attention of the importer?"

"Simon might have been tempted to send out his right-hand man to look into it. It's starting to look like our two cases may be connected."

"What do we do now?" Charlie asked.

"Tomorrow, I want you to find out everything you can on Tom Semple. Dig as deep as you can into the recesses of the web."

"Will do."

"In the meantime, I've got to puzzle out what is motivating Katherine O'Grady."

"What do you mean?" Charlie asked.

"My meeting with Gary this morning didn't yield much, other than I'm slipping up when it comes to spotting a surveillance vehicle. It turns out the police have been watching the house all week. One thought Gary planted in my brain was that Katherine just might be playing me."

"Oh. That isn't good."

"No it isn't. I hate being used. On the positive side, I've been looking into that mystery car that she photographed."

"And you found out who owns it?" Charlie asked.

"I did."

"So…who is it?"

"Florence Keough," Declan replied.

Charlie stared at him blankly. "I have no idea who that is."

"And neither do I. I just know that she is a seventy-eight-year-old woman who lives in Jasper."

"Okay. And…"

"Katherine O'Grady was certain that the car had never been on that street until the day of Archie's murder, which means either Katherine is lying, or an elderly woman was reckless enough to drive her car hundreds of kilometres down wintry roads from Jasper to Archie's street then deny doing it. Or…someone used her car, with or without her permission."

"So, what are you going to do?" Charlie asked.

"How do feel about going on a road trip to Jasper tomorrow? I want to talk to Mrs Keough in person and get to the bottom of this car business. It'll probably go better if you come along so I can take advantage of your astute observation and intuition."

"What about my background checks on Tom Semple?" Charlie asked.

"It's mostly research work, right? Bring your computer along and you can hunt for details on the mysterious Mr Semple when we've finished up with Mrs Keough. And by the way, it'll be an overnighter, so pack some clothes. Think of it as a contribution to our work–life balance. What do you say? Will you come to Jasper with me?"

Charlie smiled. "For the sake of work–life balance… Yes, boss."

Chapter Twenty-Seven

Milo looked at the clock on the wall at the Tonquin Bistro. It was twelve-thirty in the morning. All the tables had been cleared and reset for tomorrow's opening shift. Walter, the chef, poked his nose into the dining room and said, "I've got something for you."

He held out a takeout box. "I thought your cat Minx would like it. Either *she* gets it or it goes in the garbage bin."

Milo opened the container which held a generous portion of salmon. "Thanks, Walter. She'll go crazy for it."

One of the great benefits of working in a restaurant was the availability of free food. That wasn't to say it was food that was always given freely by the kitchen. Sometimes it had already been on someone else's plate. Milo figured there was no harm in taking it back to the kitchen and putting it in a doggie bag for himself. He hated to see perfectly good food go to waste. Milo decided to save the salmon for himself for lunch tomorrow. It would go well with the large glass of leftover chardonnay that he'd managed to sneak into the Thermos he always carried in his backpack.

He trudged down the main street of Jasper, which had begun to disappear under drifts of snow. A person in a heavy parka approached him. "There's been a cougar sighting up ahead. Keep your eyes peeled."

"Thanks," Milo replied.

Generally cougars avoided the town, but during the quieter winter months, it was possible for a hungry cat to wander around the deserted nighttime streets. Milo thought of the smell emanating from the box full of cooked salmon he was carrying and quickened his pace. He didn't have far to go. He cut up Aspen Avenue and turned right on Geikie Street without encountering man or beast.

When he reached the house, he removed his pack and left it inside Mrs Keough's covered porch. Then he shovelled the steps and walkway. Chores like this kept the rent on his small attic apartment low. Once he was done, he stowed the shovel away, took off his boots and entered the house.

Mrs Keough would have been in bed long before he returned from work. She always left a light on in the living room, as well as the light up the stairs. She was also considerate enough to leave the mesh fire guard around a bed of embers in the fireplace, which Milo coaxed back into flame. He sat in the chair beside the hearth. Milo liked the warmth of a fire, sitting by himself in peace, no one asking him questions. He stared into the flames. They were mesmerising. He pondered how he'd wound up in Jasper...how he had become the man he was today. His head began to droop. When he woke up, the mantle clock read a quarter to seven.

Milo quietly ran upstairs to his apartment. It was really just an attic room with an enclosed washroom in one corner. He did have a small kitchen area with a bar fridge, hot plate, coffee maker and a microwave. The only sink was in the bathroom.

Minx was sitting in the middle of the floor, and Milo could tell she was annoyed. She stared at him, then stood, turned around and sat down with her back to him.

Milo considered the cat and made a decision about what he had in his pack. "I didn't mean to be so late. But I've got a treat for you."

He refilled her water bowl, then opened his pack and pulled out the takeaway box. Minx got up and started purring, rubbing against him. It appeared the gift of salmon would undo the greatest of Milo's sins.

As she gobbled up her early morning meal, Milo sat down on the floor beside her. He lit a candle and turned off the light. He opened the Thermos and poured the wine out into one of his two tumblers. As Minx finished her fish, he reached over and gave her a scratch. She purred loudly.

"Today's a special day, Minx," he said raising his glass and pointing to the candle. "This is for Freddy. It's been ten years since he" — Milo swallowed before he finished his sentence — "died."

He looked down at the tattoo on his right calf — the initials F+M, inside a heart. Memories flooded back. The tattoos had been Milo's idea to celebrate their one-year anniversary. Milo and Freddy had met at the Calgary Stampede when they were put together in the cage of the Zipper ride. Their shared terror had sealed their bond of friendship. Before parting, they had exchanged numbers. After that, Milo had paid for Freddy to come out to Banff by bus from time to time. They would meet in a gap by the fence that surrounded The Paddock. Sometimes they would go to a movie at the Lux Cinema, sometimes they'd just take a stroll along the Bow River and sometimes they'd go for a coffee. They had to be careful who saw them. One time Milo's father had spotted them at a coffee shop. Milo had told his father that he'd just been meeting a friend from school, but he was pretty sure his father had suspected it was something else. They were more careful after that. These encounters were important. It was a time when they could both forget their home lives and live in the here and now.

His thoughts were interrupted by a loud meow. Minx looked at the candle and leaned her head toward the flame. She had a fine rack of whiskers on the left side, but she'd lost the ones on the right to a previous run-in with a candle, an incident that she'd apparently forgotten. "Stay back, you dope. You don't want to get burnt."

Milo stroked the side of her face and she purred loudly. As he pulled Minx up onto his lap he heard a gentle knock. He smiled and opened the apartment door.

"Good morning, Mrs Keough."

His landlady stood in front of him. The ponytailed, grey-haired woman was in remarkably good shape for someone in her late seventies. He had once seen her win a standoff with a black bear that had discovered the juniper berries growing in her backyard.

"I'm sorry to knock this early, but I've had a run-in with the most obstinate jam jar."

She was clutching her favourite Fortnum and Mason marmalade in her gnarled, arthritic hands, the only thing that revealed her true age.

"Let me help you with that," he said. Milo made a show of struggling to open the jar that had defeated her. "That was on pretty tight."

She took it back, then reached up and patted his cheek. "I don't know what I'd do without you, Milo."

"Anything for you, Mrs Keough," he said, then closed the door.

Milo went back to his spot on the floor and finished his wine, then blew out his candle and went to bed.

* * * *

Milo woke with a start, thrashing and gasping for air. He heard a loud hiss. His pillow was on the floor, but a moment ago, he'd been sure that someone had been holding it over his face. Milo felt something on his lips. He rubbed the back of his hand across his mouth. Orange hair. It hadn't been the pillow suffocating him...

"Minx, you are such an asshole. Can't you just bat me with your paw like a normal cat when you wanna be fed?"

He glanced at the clock on his bedside table. It was one in the afternoon. He didn't start work until four-thirty.

Milo padded his way to the sink in the bathroom and rinsed out his mouth. Minx rubbed up against his legs then started to weave in and out between them, purring loudly.

"Just wait a second. You're not gonna starve."

He pulled the remainder of the previous night's salmon out of the fridge and scooped it onto a plate, setting it gently on the floor. Minx pounced, chewing steadily through the fish.

Milo boiled a kettle of water and mixed himself an instant coffee. He poured the extra water into a bowl of instant oatmeal, then crawled back into bed. He thought back to his nightmare. He hadn't had it for months. It used to be every night. The flames. The body on the fire, then a man piling more wood on top of the flames. He could still smell it. Meat cooking. Then the dream morphed. Milo was standing on the outside looking in and a man was trying to smother him with a pillow, trying to silence him for good. Milo could still picture the look on the man's face. It was emotionless.

There was a knock at the door.

"Milo?"

"Yes, Mrs Keough?"

"I'm so sorry. I can't seem to get my car to start. Can you take a look?"

"Just give me a sec."

Milo threw on some clothes and reached for the small car battery jump-starter he had given her last year for Christmas. It had cost more than he had intended to spend, but for all she had given him, she was worth it. Unfortunately now her arthritis prevented her from attaching the clamps to the battery.

Milo smiled as he opened his door a crack. "I'll get it started for you. Oh, and don't worry about having to fill the car up with gas. I did that the other day when I borrowed it. I'll be down in a sec."

Milo closed the door, put on some socks then picked the pillow up off the floor. As he went to put it back on the bed, a heavy metal object fell out of the pillow and hit the ground.

Milo reached down and picked up the handgun, which he quickly stashed back in its hiding place. He needed to find a better place to hide the gun, but that would have to wait. Right now he had to help his unsuspecting landlady with a boost for the car he'd need to borrow again later this week.

Chapter Twenty-Eight

It was a little after one-thirty in the afternoon when Declan and Charlie entered Jasper National Park. The drive from Calgary had taken longer than expected, due to a traffic accident on the slippery highway — one of the reasons Declan had suggested that they use his van rather than Charlie's car. While the car would have been more fun for the road trip, the van had better gas mileage and weighed six hundred kilos more — weight they wanted in winter conditions in the mountains.

The forecast had been for blowing snow, so they had left Calgary early, and Declan had chosen the longer, safer route to Jasper — north on Highway 2 to just south of Edmonton, then westbound on the Yellowhead Highway coming into Jasper from the east. If the weather turned fair, perhaps they would return via the shorter route down the Icefields Parkway, but the road conditions on the high passes could be treacherous. If a winter storm descended, there was a high probability of being stuck behind a road closure, trapped in a mountain blizzard or worse, an avalanche.

Declan took a glance sideways. Charlie had fallen fast asleep, his head bobbing with the motion of the vehicle. Declan decided not to wake him as he pulled off the highway to refuel. By the time he got back in the van, Charlie was stretching his arms and stifling a yawn.

"Good morning, sleepyhead," Declan said as he started the engine.

Charlie took in his surroundings. "Wow, I had no idea it was this bad," he said, pointing to the charred remains of the forest on the edge of town, burnt during the previous summer's wildfires.

Declan nodded and pointed to the snow-covered mountains surrounding the town. "It'll take a long time to recover, but it doesn't take away from the beauty of the area. When I booked our accommodation, they were happy we were coming. The owner said whatever was burnt will come back better and stronger in the future. He said that fire cleanses the past. I don't know how people make it through their present suffering, though." They sat in silence as they drove through the town.

Ten minutes later Declan pulled into the parking lot of the Miette House Motel. Charlie got out first. Declan reached into the back seat to grab his duffle bag and felt the cardboard box.

Shit.

He'd been so preoccupied that he'd forgotten about the photo and teddy bear he'd stowed there the other day. He fished them out of the box and placed them in his bag. He'd show Charlie after they'd checked in.

"It says 'No Vacancy'," Charlie said, pointing at the sign out front.

"I booked ahead. I got the last room at the inn."

They made their way inside to the check-in desk. The young woman, who looked like she was barely out of high school, asked what name the reservation was under. After several failed attempts at spelling 'Hunt', she finally found their booking. "It only has a single king-sized bed. I'm not sure if you were told about that when you booked."

"That won't be a problem," Declan said with a smile.

"Oh. I see," she said as she winked at them. "Enjoy your time in Jasper."

They made their way to the room, which was decorated in basic boring. It had a plaid green rug on a black and white tiled floor, panel-board walls and a tourist poster of Whistler Mountain over the bed.

"Ah. I see you spared no expense and reserved us the 'mountain rustic' suite," Charlie said.

"This trip's on my dime," Declan replied. "I don't have a rich client like you."

He looked at Charlie and gave him his best leer, then reached into his duffle bag, pulled out a pair of handcuffs and threw Charlie on the bed. "What do you say we test out the mattress?"

"Shouldn't we be getting over to Mrs Keough's before it gets too late?" Charlie asked.

"It's only two in the afternoon and she's not expecting us."

Charlie smiled. "I suppose, all work and no play…"

Declan started to take off Charlie's clothes. "Let me show you a trick an old friend of mine, Martin, taught me. I think you're gonna like it."

* * * *

Declan rolled over and looked at the clock. It was three p.m.

Charlie started to stir. "I'm starving."

Declan burst out laughing. "You're always starving."

"How can you *not* be hungry after a workout like that?" Charlie asked.

"We ate in Edson, and that was only a few hours ago. Look, we passed a coffee shop down the street. If I get you a coffee and a donut, can you hold off 'til dinner?"

Charlie pouted. "I guess."

"Good, but first I want to check in with Mrs Keough before it gets too late."

After a quick shower, they drove the short distance to the Geikie Street address and pulled up in front of the brown clapboard house.

"I'll take the lead," Declan said as they made their way past a grey Impala that was tethered to the house by the telltale electrical cord of a block heater—an Alberta car owner's best friend in the winter.

Declan entered the enclosed porch then rapped the knocker on the front door.

There was no response. Declan knocked again.

He turned and shrugged at Charlie. "We'll wait back in the van and see if anyone comes home."

Just then the deadbolt was drawn back. A spry-looking older woman, barely reaching Declan's shoulders in height, opened the door. She was nicely dressed, like she was preparing to go out.

"Yes. May I help you gentlemen?" she asked.

"Mrs Florence Keough?"

"Yes." She hesitated. "Look, if this is about the fellow who bumped into my car in the shopping plaza yesterday, he was totally at fault and he admitted it on the spot. And it was just a little ding and I don't plan on pursuing it any further."

"Actually, it has nothing to do with that, but it does have to do with your car."

"Oh?"

"My name's Declan Hunt and this is my partner Charlie Watts. I spoke to you on the phone yesterday. As I said, we're looking into a case involving a murder in Calgary and we wanted to talk to you in person. Do you have a few minutes?"

"My goodness, this must be serious if you came all the way up here."

"Do you mind if we come in?"

She frowned. "Do you have some sort of ID?"

Declan handed her his private investigator's licence. She looked it over closely and handed it back.

"Will this take long? The house is a mess, but I can answer your questions right here."

"That's fine," Declan replied. "When I spoke to you and asked if your car was in Calgary last Thursday, you said no."

He pulled out his phone, "But this picture seems to show your car, the same one that's over there" — he pointed to the Impala on the street — "parked in Forest Lawn near where the murder happened last Thursday."

She rubbed the knuckles of her left hand with the thumb of her other hand. "Last Thursday, or the Thursday before?"

"Last Thursday," Declan answered.

She paused then nodded her head. "Oh, last Thursday. I thought you meant the week before when I talked to you on the phone. I get my weeks mixed up sometimes. Yes, I was in Calgary last Thursday."

Declan smiled to put her at ease. "Do you remember where you went when you were there?"

She leaned against the door jamb. "I like to get out now and then. I'd go crazy sitting here all winter, so I headed down to the big city. I was meeting a friend who recommended a coffee shop off Sixteenth Avenue, but it was busy and I had trouble parking, so I parked a street over."

"And who is this friend?" Charlie asked.

"An old school chum. I was born and raised in Calgary and went to school in the south-east part of the city. God, it sure has changed. The trees just keep on growing, sprouting up like kids—"

"Mrs Keough," Declan interrupted, "Does anyone else have access to your car?"

She crossed her arms. "Nope. Just me. Sorry to have caused you any trouble. Now, if you don't mind, I have to get going. I have dinner to prepare before I do my volunteer shift at the Legion and I'm running late."

She quickly shut the door in their faces.

Declan and Charlie returned to the van. Once he was back in the driver's seat, Declan fired up the engine and put the heater on full blast. He turned to Charlie. "She's lying through her teeth."

Charlie nodded. "Do you *think*?"

Declan said, "Her hands are stiff with arthritis. My aunt was like that and she couldn't hold onto a steering wheel for long distances, only short trips in the car. And did you have a look around the porch? There were two pairs of snow boots on the mat inside the door. One that

I was certain were hers, and a second pair that would have been big on me. And they were wet. I'll bet you anything that Mrs Keough did not drive to Calgary last week, but the owner of that second pair of boots may have."

Declan put the van into gear and drove down the road, turning around in an intersection, then returned part-way back down the street, facing Florence Keough's house.

He reached into his pocket, pulled out his wallet and handed Charlie two twenties. "Back there at the intersection, just down the street on the right, is a coffee shop. Grab us a couple of coffees and something to eat. We might be here for a bit. And keep your phone on. If we have to leave in a hurry, I'll try to pick you up. Otherwise, stay put until I can come and get you."

Chapter Twenty-Nine

Milo headed downstairs, dressed for work. He preferred the evening shift over lunch. The food was pricier and the clients drank more, which meant the tips would be better, especially if he flirted a bit. And it didn't matter if it was a man or a woman, Milo could tell by how their eyes grazed over his body if he'd get a good tip. Not that they hit on him. Not often. And it wasn't like they'd be able to track him down outside the restaurant. The name tag he wore on his uniform never carried his real name. His tag read "Mark". That was the owner's idea. She thought it would give the staff another level of security in case the clientele got a little too drawn toward one of her servers. Security or not, the owner did know the value of sex appeal. She was the one who chose the uniforms which accentuated chests and bottoms.

As he turned toward the front door, he walked by the entrance to the living room. Mrs Keough was sitting in her chair in front of the fire.

"I'll bring some more wood in when I come home," he said. "By the way, who were those guys that were just here?"

"They said they were private investigators," she replied, staring into the blazing fire. "One of them phoned yesterday when you were at work. He seemed to be very interested in why my car was in Calgary last week. Apparently it was spotted near a crime scene." She looked up at him. "Initially I thought it was a mistake, but today they showed me a picture and it was definitely my car. I covered for you, Milo, but it does have me wondering why you drove all the way down to Calgary and parked on a street in Forest Lawn."

Milo walked into the living room. "You said I could borrow the car anytime I wanted. I know Calgary's a long ways away but I made sure that I filled up the tank as soon as I got back and I'll give you some money for maintenance—how about if I pay for the next tune-up? It would only be fair."

"Milo, dear, I don't mind you using the car. You can drive it to Saskatoon if you want. I just hope that you're not mixed up in anything bad."

He smiled and sat on the ottoman near her. "I just went down to visit a guy I met at the restaurant. We've been chatting back and forth. I didn't want to tell you because…well, it's personal."

"A new beau?" she replied. "Must be something special to drive all that way. Have you been more than once?"

He gave her a lopsided grin and shrugged his shoulders. "Maybe."

She turned to him. "Well, as long as you filled up the tank with gas. I lied to those detectives because I wanted to find out the truth from you first, but if it's really nothing and they ask again, I might have to be honest with them. Understood?"

"Yes, ma'am."

* * * *

Declan had turned off the engine for the stakeout and was beginning to notice just how poorly insulated his van was. This was the unglamorous part of being a private investigator—sitting, watching, waiting for someone to do something. And in Alberta in winter, it usually involved freezing his nuts off.

The door of the house opened and a body bundled up in a coat made their way to the street. And it wasn't Mrs Keough.

Declan started his engine, put the heater on full then pulled out his cell phone.

"Hello," Charlie answered.

"Where are you? I have a body on the move."

The van door opened and Charlie slid in.

"Some detective you are. What if I'd had a knife?" Charlie asked.

"I'd have done this," he said, stepping on the gas and throwing Charlie back in his seat.

"Hey. I've got coffees!"

Declan reached over and took one. "Thanks."

"So, who do we have? I'm assuming it's not Mrs Keough?"

"Not sure, but I'm pretty sure it's the owner of the large boots. Let's see where they're going."

* * * *

Charlie and Declan carefully followed the person who had left Mrs Keough's. The suspect strode confidently around the corner and headed toward Jasper Avenue. As Declan's van approached the main street, traffic started to build and their suspect started to gain ground. Charlie said, "I'm getting out. I'll follow them on foot. If they pop into some place while we're backed up in traffic, we'll lose them."

Without waiting for Declan to respond, Charlie slipped out of the van and hurried down the street. As he got closer, Charlie was able to make out that the suspect appeared to be a young man. He was moving fast. And who could blame him? It was fucking cold out. Charlie's 'going for a car ride' sneakers weren't the best footwear for the job. He prayed that this guy would reach his destination before Charlie froze his toes off.

Charlie rounded a corner and saw the man walk up to the side door of a restaurant. He kicked his boots against the wall, dislodging the snow they carried, then flipped back the hood of his parka and went in.

The young man had shoulder-length black hair.

Coincidence?

Charlie waited fifteen minutes, then went around to the front of the restaurant. The person of interest was serving tables inside.

Charlie looked around, then pulled out his cell phone and called Declan. "I know where we're going to eat tonight. I'll be in front of the Christmas Store next to a restaurant called the Tonquin Bistro. You can't miss it."

Declan pulled up and Charlie hopped in.

"Christ, you must be frozen," Declan said.

"Would it be bad to pour coffee on my feet?"

"You just need to get inside someplace warm," Declan replied. "You said you were hungry. Shall we go for dinner now?"

"I thought you'd never ask."

Declan parked the van and they made their way to the entrance of the restaurant. The Tonquin Bistro was plainer than the name suggested – a faux log structure designed to fit the town's architectural theme. Charlie wondered if it was designed to mimic the Jasper Park Lodge, the grand-dame of Jasper hotels not far away. Perhaps if it looked like the lodge, the food would be as good.

Through the window, he saw the young man with the long dark hair. He was dressed in a white shirt, tight-fitting black trousers and a matching black vest, as was the young woman he was standing with.

"You go in first," Declan said. "Make sure you're seated in his section and try to get a feel for what he's about. I'll join you in a few minutes."

Charlie went in and soon found himself seated at a table.

"Hello," the server said. "My name is Mark and I'll be taking care of you this evening. Will you be dining by yourself?"

"Uh...no," Charlie stuttered. *Stop looking at his crotch!* "A friend will be joining us, I mean me." Charlie didn't know what else to do, so he moved his glance upward which didn't help. Mark had the most beautiful emerald-green eyes.

"Very good. May I bring you a drink while you wait?" The server leaned in and added softly in Charlie's ear, "Don't fall for any of the upper-end vintages. They're not worth the price and most people can't tell the difference from the house wines." He punctuated the sentence with a wink.

"Well then, I'll start with a glass of the house red and we'll see what my partner – friend," he quickly corrected, "will have when he gets here."

Mark brought him the glass of wine and a tray of appetisers. "Smoked salmon bites and olives. On the house."

"Thank you," Charlie said, thinking that he would come here more often if it wasn't such a long drive away.

Mark smiled, then bowed discreetly and left Charlie in peace.

As the restaurant began to fill up, Mark brought Charlie over a glass of water, slipping it above the cutlery to his right. Charlie was sure that as he was departing, the server flexed his buttocks. After almost an entire glass of wine, he didn't mind for an instant. It was clear that the server knew how to get good tips.

The door to the restaurant opened and Declan walked in.

Charlie stood and raised his hand slightly so that Declan could see where he was. Declan passed the host his coat, which was immediately hung in a closet. *Why did I bring mine to the table? I look like such an idiot.*

As the detective made his way across the room, all eyes were on him and his glorious physique. He got to the table and made no attempt to hide the kiss he laid on Charlie's lips.

The server was there in an instant to pull out Declan's chair and seat him.

Declan looked up at him, "Thank you…?"

"Mark," both the server and Charlie answered in unison.

"I'll have what Charlie's having," Declan said, pointing to his glass.

"Certainly."

"And I'll have another," Charlie said.

Once the server had left them, Declan asked, "So, how's it going? Any feelings as to what this guy is all about? It is the guy we followed from Mrs Keough's place isn't it?"

"Oh, it's him, all right and he's spent every moment he's been around flirting up a storm. It's interesting. He matches the description the kid from Banff gave of the guy who paid him to deliver the note to Simon. But it doesn't look like the aged-up photo of Milo."

"Maybe it's someone who's working with him," Declan offered.

Charlie shrugged. "Where do we go from here?"

"No need to rush," Declan replied. "He's not going anywhere. Let's enjoy dinner."

When Mark returned, Declan asked for a recommendation and ordered a Swiss fondue with coffee and dessert.

The server was attentive, and when the meal was finished, Mark returned and asked, "I hope everything was to your liking?"

"It couldn't have been better. Thank you, Mark."

"Then will there be anything else, gentlemen? An after-dinner drink, perhaps?"

"No, I'm afraid we have to hit the road," Declan replied.

"I hope you don't have to drive too far. The weather looks like it'll be a bit treacherous tonight."

"All the way back to Calgary, I'm afraid."

Mark raised his eyebrows. "Oh."

"Have you been down there?" Declan asked.

"A few times, but never in conditions like this. And certainly not at night. My car wouldn't take it."

A grey Impala, perhaps, Charlie thought.

"So, were you born here in Jasper?" Declan continued.

"No. Long story," Mark said. "Not very interesting. Well, we'd better get you back on the road."

"Yeah. Work calls," Declan replied.

"And what sort of work are you in?"

Charlie answered, "We're private investigators."

It was all Charlie had to say. The smile dropped off of Mark's face.

"I'll bring you your bill. Will that be all on one?"

Declan said, "That would be fine. Thanks." He gave the server what would have been a heart-melting smile, except Mark was a little preoccupied at the moment. Charlie doubted it had anything to do with the bill.

Mark left the table and headed to the corner of the restaurant where he started an intense discussion with a beautiful young female server who kept looking over at their table. Declan discretely snapped a picture of their server with his phone then turned to Charlie. "What's wrong? You look upset."

"I thought we were going to spend the night in the hotel," Charlie said.

"Oh, we are. I just told him we were leaving tonight to keep him on edge. Did you see how he reacted when you told him we were private investigators? He's hiding something. I can't wait to see what he does when we show up on his doorstep tomorrow."

Charlie said, "Should we wait that long?"

"I don't see that there's any rush. He thinks we're leaving town. In the meantime, you can use your computer to see if the picture I took matches any persons of interest online."

Declan looked out of the window. "The weather's closing in. I don't think he's going anywhere tonight, and neither are we."

Chapter Thirty

Charlie woke up. Something wasn't right. He wasn't where he thought he should be. Charlie shook his head and got out of bed. His feet took him downstairs and into Declan's office.

What the fuck?

He heard a sound, like a tinkling bell.

Ting-ting-ting.

It seemed to be coming from the main room of the office.

Ting-ting-ting.

It was getting louder. He poked his head out of the door and saw Dave the ghost walking toward him. He stared at Charlie, stirring his cup of coffee.

Ting-ting-ting.

Dave looked much worse for wear.

Charlie was surprised that seeing the ghost no longer sent him into fits of terror. Dave raised his cup to Charlie, then walked past him and into Declan's office. Charlie followed. In between the *tinging* of his spoon against the cup, Dave was humming a tune. It was the Baby Bunting lullaby. Charlie's brain filled in the words. "Bye, Baby Bunting. Daddy's gone a-hunting." Each phrase was followed by a *ting-ting-ting*. Dave hummed the tune over and over again as he walked slowly around Declan's office, followed by Charlie. Dave seemed to be looking for something. He stopped, then made his way over to the credenza. He picked up the photo of Freddy Whitcher and held it out to Charlie.

"Come and find me," he whispered, then Dave started to change. What was left of his face grew older, wrinkled, then dissolved into thin air.

Charlie woke with a start. He was panting heavily. He was no longer in Declan's office. It was a bedroom, but not his. It took a moment before he realised that it was the room at the Miette House Motel. It was dark, and there was no trace of Dave.

"Fuck," he whispered, settling back down into his pillow. He turned his head. Declan was sound asleep, mouth open, breathing in a semi-snore. A small trickle of drool hung from the corner of his mouth.

Charlie stared up at the ceiling.

What the fuck was that dream about?

He hadn't dreamt of Dave for a few nights, and that song — crap, it was like something out of a horror film. Dreams of ghosts, hunting, people getting younger and older... This case was obviously getting to him.

Charlie couldn't get back to sleep. He pondered his dream. Dave had held up Freddy's picture. *What did he say this time?* "Come and find me." Then he —

"Declan," Charlie whispered. He didn't want to startle him awake. "Declan," he repeated, gently rubbing his shoulder.

"Mmmpf." Declan said as his eyes opened. "Something wrong?" he asked, slowly rolling over.

"Declan. Do you have a copy of the picture of Freddy on your phone?"

"What?" Declan asked, shaking his head.

"I need a copy of the picture of Freddy. The one from your office." Charlie spoke slowly so Declan's sleepy brain might understand. "Do you have a copy on your phone?"

"Why?"

Declan sounded more awake.

"I have an idea that I want to test but I need that picture."

Declan sighed. "Actually, I can do you one better." He slid slowly out of bed, picked up his duffle bag and put it on the dresser. He reached in and extracted a framed photo of Freddy, and handed it to Charlie. "Will this do? I borrowed it from Katherine O'Grady. I can't believe I didn't show it to you earlier."

"I think that'll work."

Charlie put the framed photo on the desk and snapped a picture of it with his phone, then sent it to his computer. He opened up his laptop and retrieved the picture from his email, then pressed the icon for the BenButton app and uploaded Freddy's photo. It took a minute to follow the software prompts, identifying the year that the original image had been taken, as well as the age of the person depicted at the time. Charlie guessed fourteen. He asked it to age him to a twenty-four-year-old from Jasper, Alberta, Canada. Middle class.

Charlie pressed the button labelled "Age me".

Declan stood behind him, holding onto his shoulders.

In seconds, an image popped up on the screen. Charlie let out a low whistle. He went back into the program and altered the colour and length of the hair and ran the process again. Staring back at him was a very close match to the server from the Tonquin Bistro.

Declan tightened his grip on Charlie's shoulders. "It's *got* to be a mistake," Declan said. "Freddy is dead. He died in a fire ten years ago."

Charlie turned. Declan's face had gone pale. Charlie said, "Let me try again. Maybe there's some distortion from the glass in front of the photo. Can you take the picture out of the frame and we'll try one more time?"

* * * *

Declan flipped the picture over and started to remove the backing of the frame. It took a bit of effort because the board was tightly wedged. When he finally got the backing off, he discovered the reason it was held in place so tightly. The photo in the four-by-five frame was actually an eight-by-ten that had been folded to fit… Or folded to hide what the full picture showed.

Charlie uttered a quiet, "What the…"

The complete photo showed two boys sitting side by side. The boy on the left was clearly Milo at a similar age to the picture provided by Simon Griffin. The boy on the right was Freddy. Milo had a teddy bear sitting on his lap, the teddy bear that was resting in Declan's bag. The boys were wearing shorts. Both of them had similar crudely inked tattoos on their calves. Milo's had the initials M+F surrounded by a heart. Freddy's had the initials F+M, surrounded by a similar heart. It was clear the tattoos were different. The initials were in a different order.

Declan quickly reached for his phone and pulled up the photographs from the police files that Gary Sawchuck had shared. One of those photos was of the leg that had been found after the fire, an image that Declan had carried around in his head for ten years, but he had to be sure. The tattoo in the heart on the leg in the police photo clearly said M+F.

Declan swore. "It can't be. Archie identified his son. How could he not recognise the difference?"

Charlie shrugged. "Maybe on the day he identified him, he was upset. He probably hadn't taken a close look at the tattoo—he just knew they were initials in a heart and that they were an M and an F. Do you remember, did he spend long at the morgue?"

Declan cast his mind back to that day. "He was still sobering up. He was a mess. I don't think he was there more than ten minutes."

Declan sat down on the bed and looked at the photo again.

"I spent the last ten years trying to get some justice for Freddy. My career was built on that kid. Whenever I was ready to give up, I thought of him. Now I find out that Freddy is alive and it was all a lie."

Charlie put his hand on Declan's shoulder. "You didn't become who you were because of Freddy. You did it because of what happened to him before you thought he died. And right now we need to find out what really happened. Are you going to be all right?"

Declan took a deep breath. "How I'm feeling doesn't matter right now. We need to get to Mrs Keough's house and find out what's going on."

Chapter Thirty-One

The questions the detectives had asked at the restaurant had unnerved Milo... No, not Milo. It was time to undo the past—to correct the lies. At work he was Mark. At Mrs Keough's he was Milo, but over ten years ago, he had been Freddy.

He looked at the tattoo on his leg and remembered what had led to Freddy becoming Milo.

It had started ten years ago when Freddy's father Archie had been drinking a lot. Freddy had come out of the bathroom after showering. He had only been wearing a towel when Archie had seen his tattoo and asked what it was. Freddy had decided to tell his father the truth—that he was gay, he was in love and he was seeing another boy. His father had mocked him, and said that Freddy didn't know what he was talking about, and that no son of his was going to grow up to be a faggot. When Freddy had shouted back that it was too late, Archie had taken off his belt and told Freddy he would beat the gay out of him.

Freddy had tolerated the first beating, but after two weeks of trying to avoid his father and encountering his fists several nights in a row, he decided he'd had enough. Freddy had gotten in touch with Milo and told him that he was going to run away from home. To his surprise, Milo had told him that he was thinking of doing the same thing. The relationship with his father had deteriorated, and Milo had discovered something terrible. His father had killed someone. Milo had said that he had evidence that proved it. He'd told Freddy that they could run away together and explained that he had some money and knew where to get his father's car keys. Milo would come and pick Freddy up.

They never really thought it through. There was no firm plan, just an idea and the naivety of youth. Freddy had suggested they meet at an industrial park not far from his house. It was a place that wouldn't have many people around at night. The thought of it had been exhilarating. They were both going to be free.

Things hadn't gone according to plan from the beginning. As Freddy had begun to pack, his father had come into his room and started toward him. Freddy had run out of the house with little more than his wallet and a few clothes. He hadn't had time to grab the picture of him and Milo that he'd hidden beneath his mattress, nor the teddy bear that they had won at the Stampede. Freddy was upset, but there was no going back now.

Things had seemed better when he got to the industrial park and Milo was there in his dad's fancy car. Just as Milo had stepped out of the vehicle and waved, another car had pulled in to the far end of the lot. Milo had signalled Freddy to stay where he was, then he'd reached into the car, grabbed his pack and thrown it behind a nearby dumpster. Milo had looked one last time at Freddy before the other car had screeched to a halt and a man had gotten out of the driver's seat. He was angry. In the headlights Freddy could make out that the man was well-built and he had the face of a boxer…someone who had taken more than a few punches.

Milo had approached the man. It was clear that he knew him by name. It was Tom, Milo's bodyguard. Freddy had heard stories about him from Milo, most of them unpleasant. Tom had asked where Milo was going. Milo had told him to fuck off. Tom replied that Milo had made a big mistake in stealing his father's car. Milo had said that it didn't matter. It was nothing compared to what his father had done…killing a man. And he'd added he had proof, then said that he knew that Tom was involved. To this day, Freddy didn't understand why Milo had gone so far, but he understood what was going to happen next when Tom had lunged at Milo, picked him up and started to shake him. Then he had thrown Milo to the ground…hard. Milo had stopped moving. Tom had lifted Milo by the collar and had shaken him again. Milo was like a rag doll. This had infuriated Tom further and he had punched and kicked until his fury was done. It was clear that Milo was gone. Freddy wanted to run, but he was paralysed with fear and grief.

When Tom realised that Milo must be dead, he had made a quick call on his phone. Then he'd found some wooden skids and some paper from a nearby dumpster and started a fire. The wood was dry and old, and before long the fire was crackling. He had thrown the body in the middle and piled more wood on top. While the fire burnt, Tom had checked the inside of Milo's dad's car, but it was clear that he didn't find what he was looking for. He had screamed with frustration and slammed his hand on the roof of the car. Then he'd started to laugh. "Liar," he'd shouted out to the fire. "You fucking little liar. You didn't have any proof! Now look what you've done."

It was only a few minutes until two other men arrived in a truck. One of them got into Milo's dad's car and drove it away. The other followed. Freddy had watched Tom make sure that the fire was ablaze and had done its work. Tom had taken one last quick look around, then gotten into his car and driven away. The lot was empty once more. Freddy was left alone shivering in the cold.

After everyone was gone, Freddy had looked to see if he could put out the fire, but it was too late. He had to do something. He'd remembered Milo's bag and went to where it had been thrown. Inside he had found a lot of cash and clothes...and a USB key.

Instinct took over. Milo was dead. Freddy had taken Milo's bag. He'd looked at his own knapsack. There was nothing of value in it, so he'd left it behind and had run away from the lot, away from Milo and toward the downtown core of the city.

In time, Freddy had managed to walk to the bus station. He had cash in hand, so he'd bought a ticket on the next bus leaving town. He'd told the ticket vendor that he was travelling north to visit his aunt. They'd asked if he would be accompanied, and he'd told them he wouldn't, and that his mother had dropped him off. Maybe the ticket vendor had run away themselves in the past. Maybe they were kind. Or maybe they didn't care. Whatever happened that night, Freddy had gotten a ticket to Jasper.

He had landed in town early the next morning and found himself at a diner. An older waitress served his table. He could tell she'd seen the bruises on his arms, and she had said that he didn't seem very well dressed to be in Jasper in the winter. She'd asked if he was in some sort of trouble.

Freddy had told a partial truth. He'd explained that his father had been beating him, and he had run away. He had put some distance between them, but he hadn't figured out a plan beyond that. She had introduced herself as Mrs Keough, and had offered him a place to stay in exchange for doing some chores until he landed on his feet. When she'd asked him his name, he had lied. He'd said "Milo. Milo Binns". The last name was his mother's maiden name.

Freddy—now Milo—had laid low and avoided being out in case he had somehow been followed. That was when he'd seen an article in the *Calgary Herald* about a grisly find in an industrial park near Forest Lawn. The police had identified the victim as a young runaway by the name of Freddy Whitcher. He had debated going to the police, but if he told the truth, the man who had killed Milo would likely come after him. These were mobsters. Tom had killed Milo and now that Freddy's pack had been discovered at the site, he suspected that Tom might be looking for him.

Freddy had decided to stay in Jasper. The landlady had taken a shine to him and told him he could stay as long as he wanted. She'd offered to homeschool him and arranged for him to get a part-time job at the diner as a busboy. He'd worked 'under the table' for cash, a common practice at many of the restaurants that often hired foreign students who didn't have access to things like bank accounts or social insurance numbers. He liked the work and he liked Mrs. Keough. When people asked, she had said that Milo was the son of a cousin who'd come upon hard times and she was simply helping out.

Before Freddy knew it, a year had gone by. Nobody had come after him. And what would be gained by Freddy going after the mobsters? Everyone called him Milo now, and he decided that was who he would be. He would start his life again.

In time, Milo had found some friends who'd helped him with things like getting fake ID which had allowed him to open a chequing account at the bank. He'd found a way to beat the system. The money from Milo's pack, which he had hidden away in various places around his room, was slowly deposited month by month into his account. He'd made sure to let Mrs Keough know that he was capable of keeping his room tidy, even doing his own laundry, so there was less of a chance of her stumbling on his stash of cash. He truly felt like he had established a new life in Jasper.

Then, a month ago, he had seen the pictures of the real Milo's dad's house in the *Rocky Mountain Leisure* magazine. Had Simon Griffin ever thought of his missing son? Had his henchman, Tom, told Simon that his son was dead? And if so, did his father even care? The grief and pain returned, as had something new — rage!

Freddy had made a plan. He had talked to the friends who had helped him with fake ID. They were able to help him secure a gun. He had waited until Mrs. Keough was away for a week visiting her sister in Edmonton, then borrowed her car, making his way down to Banff, Canmore and Calgary…twice. He'd wanted to start making Mr Griffin and the man who had killed Milo squirm. He'd wanted them to know that someone knew what they had done.

* * * *

Freddy sat at his small kitchen table. Minx jumped up in his lap.

"You're not helping, you know."

He scrubbed Minx under the chin and she settled down in his lap. Freddy took a sip of his coffee and picked up a pen and began to write a letter.

Dear Mrs Keough...

When he was finished, he packed up all of his clothes, along with a few mementos. Then he wrapped his handgun in a towel and tucked it deep into his bag. After taking one last look around, he went down the stairs and got in the car. It was time to finish this once and for all.

Chapter Thirty-Two

Declan pulled the van in front of Mrs. Keough's at a little after seven in the morning. He pointed to the electrical cord neatly wrapped beside the house. It wasn't attached to anything. "Car's gone."

He knocked loudly on the front door as Charlie stepped into the covered porch. Mrs Keough answered the door. She was fully dressed.

"Do you know where Freddy is?" Declan asked.

"Freddy? Who's that?"

"The young man that was staying here," Declan replied.

"Oh, there must be some confusion. There's no Freddy here. My tenant's name is Milo."

She started to close the door but Declan put his hand in the way. "Please, Mrs Keough, this is urgent. We need to speak to him right now."

"Look—I heard him bustling about early this morning. He's probably gone in for an early shift at the restaurant."

"I don't think that's it," Declan said. "Your car's gone, and I doubt he's taken it to work. Do you mind if we have a look at his room? It might give us a clue as to where he's gone. He's in big trouble and we want to help him."

She stared at Declan intently. "Maybe he's still up there. I'll go check his room, but I'm sure everything's okay." She turned and headed up the stairs.

Declan and Charlie stepped into the front hall, closing the door behind them. Without waiting to be asked they kicked off their boots and followed her. She reached the attic at the top of the stairs and knocked on the door. "Milo, are you in there? There are some gentlemen here who say they need to talk to you."

There was no response. She tried the door but it was locked.

"Do you have a key?" Charlie asked.

"Just a minute." She scuttled back down the stairs and returned shortly. Mrs Keough inserted a key into the lock and opened the door. There was nobody there except for an orange-haired cat that gave a low growl as they entered the room.

Declan turned to Mrs Keough. "Is there anything missing or out of place?"

She walked around the small space and opened the cupboard in the corner. "His clothes are all gone."

She moved to the kitchen table and picked up an envelope that had been left behind. "It's addressed to me."

She opened it and pulled out a folded piece of paper which she read out loud.

Dear Mrs Keough,
I want you to know just how much I appreciate everything you've done since you found me all those years ago. You helped me start a new life. One a lot better than I had.

I think the time has come for me to move on. Since I'm not sure when, or where, I'll be settling down next, I don't think it would be fair to Minx to take her along with me. I know she loves you, and I hope you will take care of her.

Years ago I deposited $6000 in a chequing account. I've left a cheque here for you in that amount. I hope it's enough to buy you a new used car, because I've had to borrow yours again. Kind of permanently.

Something has come up and I've realised that if I want to be able to live with myself, I have to fix the past.

Please don't call the police and report me missing.

Tons of love,

Milo.

She looked in the envelope again and pulled out a second piece of paper. It was the cheque.

She reread the letter. "What do you think he means when he says he has to fix the past if he wants to live with himself?"

Declan scowled. "It means we have to stop him from doing something stupid."

"May I see the letter?" Charlie asked. She passed it to him. He studied the note and thrust it toward Declan. "See the weird way the capital I is written? It's the same as on the note Simon received. I'm sure of it."

"So he's probably headed to The Paddock," Declan said.

Declan quickly ran down the stairs with Charlie close on his heels. They jumped into the van leaving behind a bewildered Mrs Keough.

"What do we do now?" Charlie asked.

"See if you can get Simon Griffin on the phone and tell him not to let anyone into the house except for us."

* * * *

The sun was starting to peek over the mountains as Freddy made his way south on the Icefields Parkway. It was obvious that the maintenance staff had been out early as the road was freshly sanded. At first, the signs of last year's massive fire were everywhere, but as Freddy drove toward Banff, the evidence of the tragedy faded behind him. It was a beautiful day, unlike the past two times he'd come this way.

The first time, nine days ago, the weather had been snowy and he'd had to drive slowly. He hadn't gotten to Banff until late in the afternoon. By the time he had found parking and convinced a kid to deliver a note to Simon's house, the sun had almost set. After Freddy had watched the note being delivered, he'd gone back to the car and discovered that the engine wouldn't turn over. He had cursed himself for not bringing the battery jump-starter he'd given Mrs Keough. It had been too late to drive back to Jasper anyway, and Mrs Keough wasn't going to be back until next Tuesday, so he'd opted to leave the car parked on the street and stay overnight in Banff. There was something delicious about being so close to The Paddock with Milo's father not knowing he was there.

The following morning, Freddy had managed to find someone to give him a boost, but the weather was still cold and snowy. Rather than taking the Icefields Parkway back, Freddy had opted to travel east to Calgary and take the safer route up Highway 2. He didn't have to be back to work until the following morning. He still had time.

As he'd made his way to the edge of Calgary, an impulse had taken a hold of him. He'd wanted to see where it had all begun. Freddy hadn't been home since he'd first fled the city. He had pictured the shock on his father's face if he walked up to the front door, rang the doorbell and said, "Hey, guess what, Dad? I'm not dead. How does that make you feel?" But he never got the chance.

He had managed to park on the street, but before he'd gotten out of the car, Freddy had seen a man in a long brown coat leave by the front door of Freddy's old home. The man was moving in a hurry. Then a woman had come out onto the street. She was looking around, and Freddy had ducked to ensure she didn't see him. Something had seemed off. That was when he'd heard sirens. It was too much. Freddy had gotten out of there as fast as he could and made his way back to Jasper.

It wasn't until a few days later that Freddy had read in the *Calgary Herald* that there'd been a homicide. The newspaper had identified the victim as his father, Archie Whitcher. Freddy had thought about the man he'd seen leaving the house. He was pretty sure he knew who he was.

I bet you killed him, you psycho.

The man in the brown coat seemed very much like the man who had killed Milo. He had a distinctive build. It had to be the guy Milo had called Tom.

After Freddy had gotten back to Jasper, he'd realised that Mrs Keough wasn't going to be back for a few more days, so he'd planned a second trip to Banff.

He'd called in sick to work, retrieved his gun and driven the Icefields Parkway once more, arriving in Banff near the dinner hour. The drive had been fair, as a Chinook had been blowing that afternoon. Freddy had sat in his car on the street and watched The Paddock as he'd tried to pluck up his courage to act. He was trying to make up his mind what to do when Simon Griffin had driven out of the property, and headed east. Freddy had followed him to a restaurant fifteen minutes away, and luck was with him. Tom had arrived and parked right beside Simon's car. Freddy had waited until they were both inside the restaurant. He had taken great joy in putting a big scratch in Milo's father's Bentley, then left a note on both cars that was a little more threatening than the first. It was too public a place to try anything more. Instead, he would come back on the day he had first planned, closer to the tenth anniversary of Milo's death and bring this situation to an end. He would stick to his original plan.

He'd made the long drive home that night, arriving before Mrs. Keough got back to Jasper, in time for his morning shift.

And that brought him to today. It didn't even matter that there were detectives asking questions. Freddy took in the beautiful mountain scenery around him and smiled. If it went badly at The Paddock, at least he would have this last glorious memory to hold onto. Things had been put into action that could not be undone.

Chapter Thirty-Three

Declan drove as quickly as the roads would allow. They made it to Banff in three and a half hours. As they approached The Paddock, Declan and Charlie kept their eyes peeled for Freddy's car, but there was no sign of it.

"Maybe he parked on another street," Charlie offered.

"We'll see."

Declan pulled up to the gates, leaned out and pushed the intercom button.

A voice said, "Yes."

Charlie leaned past Declan. "Mr Griffin, it's Charlie Watts. Can you let us in please?"

The gate slowly opened and Declan parked the van. There were two other cars already in the drive. As they walked to the front door, it opened.

"Tom," Charlie said extending his hand. "This is Declan Hunt."

"Simon's in the living room," Tom said, as he led Declan and Charlie inside.

"So, you must be the famous Declan Hunt. It's a pleasure to meet you," Simon said, standing and reaching out to shake Declan's hand.

"Mr Griffin," Declan acknowledged.

"Please, take a seat. May I offer you a coffee or tea? My housekeeper Jasmine is off for the day, but I'm sure I can figure out how to use that fancy silver machine in the kitchen. *Or*, if it's not too early for you, I could offer you a real drink."

"I think we're fine," Declan answered for both of them as he and Charlie sat side by side on a wide leather couch at the side of the room.

Simon sat down on a chair to their right. Tom sat in a chair opposite Simon.

He wants to keep an eye on all of us, Declan thought.

Simon broke the ice. "So what is this all about?"

Charlie started. "Simon, we've found Milo, but the news isn't good. And we think that you may be at risk from the person who wrote the note."

Simon sat back in his chair. "From the way you worded that, I assume the person who wrote the note *wasn't* Milo?"

Charlie said, "No, it wasn't." He glanced at Declan before he continued, "When your son disappeared, you said that he was seeing a young man, and you said you didn't know his name. Have you ever heard of a person by the name of Freddy Whitcher, or his father Archie?"

Simon's brow furrowed. "The name sounds vaguely familiar. Now why would I know that name?"

"Well," Charlie replied, "Freddy Whitcher was the boy who was seeing your son when he disappeared."

"Oh. I see," Simon said.

"And Archie Whitcher might sound familiar because it was reported in the Calgary papers that he was murdered just over a week ago."

"That's probably it. But what does all of this have to do with Milo?"

Charlie cleared his throat. "Well, it seems that around ten years ago, the newspapers reported that the boy your son was seeing, Freddy Whitcher, died in a fire. But we know now that the boy that died in the fire wasn't Freddy... It was Milo."

Simon's face remained emotionless. "So, you're saying my son is dead?"

"Yes," Charlie replied.

"And do you have proof?" Simon asked.

Declan reached into the bag he'd brought, and pulled out the photograph of the two boys—the one he'd borrowed from Katherine O'Grady. He passed it to Simon. "Have you ever seen this photo of your son and Freddy?"

Simon looked at the picture closely. "I haven't seen *this* picture. But it's interesting...the boy on the right, when I was at your office, there was a picture of him on the credenza, wasn't there?"

"Yes. I was with the Calgary Police at the time. I was the one who found what remained of a boy's body. All that was clearly identifiable was a leg with a tattoo."

"And you kept his picture?" Tom interjected. "Rather macabre."

Declan turned to him. "That case impacted me deeply and I kept the boy's picture to remind myself why the work I do is important...to help the young and defenceless." He turned back to Simon. "The boy was identified by his father based on the tattoo on his leg, but it wasn't the right tattoo. If you look closely at this photo you'll see that the tattoos on their legs are similar, but not identical. The tattoo of the boy burnt in the fire matches the one on Milo's leg."

Simon frowned. "So who sent the threatening note then?"

A sound behind them indicated that someone had just entered the room.

"That would be me."

"And who the hell are you?" Simon yelled.

"Freddy Whitcher," Declan said.

Freddy stood at the entrance to the living room. He had a gun in his hand and it was aimed directly at Tom. "I would have been here sooner, but I stopped to get gas and the battery conked out on my car. I see you've got company, Mr Griffin," he said, pointing at Declan and Charlie. "I guess there's no harm in them hearing what I've got to say."

"And that is?" Simon asked.

Freddy sneered. "Well, first of all, you may be interested to know that your friend Tom over there knew that your son was dead all along. In fact, he's the one who killed him."

Simon's eyes widened. "Is that true, Tom?"

Tom's face was still, but his eyes turned a shade darker. "No, Simon. He's lying. You know I looked far and wide for Milo. On the night he ran away, we used the tracking device on your car and we found it at the airport. There was no Milo. And then he just disappeared."

Freddy laughed. "Well, the car may have wound up at the airport after your friends moved it, but first it came to an industrial park in Forest Lawn to pick me up."

Freddy turned to Simon. "Milo and I were running away that night. But Tom here got in the way."

Freddy moved closer to Tom.

Declan stood. "Freddy, don't do anything stupid."

Freddy pivoted toward Declan pointing the gun at him. "You stay out of this."

He turned back to Tom. "You see, Tom, when you arrived, Milo spotted you and waved at me to hide. I watched as you beat the life out of him. I watched as you piled wood around him and lit the fire. And I watched as you drove away. I was sure you would come after me, but you never saw me, did you?"

Tom smiled coldly, "You're making this up. What do you want? Is it money? If this is blackmail, Simon has lots of money."

Freddy said, "Oh no, I don't want money. I want justice."

Tom started to rise from his chair and Freddy took another step toward him. "By the way, Tom, what was it you were looking for on the night you murdered Simon's son? Anything particular? Because you checked the car. I saw you. And you weren't happy when you didn't find it." He took another step closer. "What did Milo have that you wanted so badly?"

Tom said, "I didn't look for anything. I just wanted Milo to come home."

Freddy nodded. "Ah, so you admit you were there?"

Tom's neck muscles tensed.

He's not going to take this much longer, Declan thought.

Freddy continued, "Simon, I should let you know, you can't really trust Tom. He didn't do a very good job. Not only did he kill your son, but he left behind something Milo had hidden in a backpack. It was right behind the dumpster Tom got the paper from to start the fire."

Simon folded his hands. "And what exactly was in the backpack, young man?"

"Money. Lots of it…and a USB key that has a rather interesting conversation recorded on it. Does the name Roger Feist mean anything to you?"

The edges of Simon's lips began to twitch.

Who the hell is Roger Feist? Declan thought.

Freddy continued. "I don't know how, but somehow when you were on a call on speakerphone in your office, Milo managed to record it. You can clearly hear someone say that if you sent your man Tom here to kill Roger Feist—the son of the head of Monarch Holdings apparently—"

Monarch! Declan shot Charlie a glance. It was clear from the pallor of his face that he had also clocked the name of the company.

" — that the person on the other end of the call would help you acquire some sort of relic. It was all highly illegal, of course, but something you apparently wanted badly. It was quite a lively call."

Simon put his hands in the pockets of his sweater. "I think you're lying."

Freddy said, "I assure you, I'm not. For a long time, I was afraid of your organisation, but after ten years, it's time to put things right. You might be interested to know I looked up Roger Feist's father. It appears he's heavily involved in real estate, and it was pretty easy to get a number for a secretary that could pass him a message. She gave me a phone number with an answering machine. I didn't leave a long message. I just said that I was phoning, anonymously of course, to let him know that Simon Griffin was responsible for the death of his son. And that the person who had killed him was Tom Semple. And then I mailed his office a copy of the USB key. I don't know if he got or not. Probably not yet, but he will soon."

Tom lunged toward Freddy. "You little fucker."

Freddy pulled the trigger on the gun. The bullet tore open the floor near Tom's feet. It stopped him in his tracks.

"Freddy. Put the gun down," Declan ordered, but Freddy didn't waver.

"You think you know so much, kid," Tom sneered. "You don't know the half of it. After I saw the article about Freddy Whitcher's supposed death, I put two and two together. I tracked down your father and staked out his house for close to a year after you disappeared, but you never came home. I had a hunch that Milo might have said something to his little boyfriend, but you were like a ghost in the wind. And then last week when that note showed up, I knew I must have missed something."

Tom clenched his fists and shifted his weight from one foot to the other. He looked like he was about to explode.

"So, last week I went back to the house, I went inside and I asked your father if he'd seen his son. He started to cry, saying his son was dead, but I didn't buy it, not for a second. I figured he must have known where you were, and I thought I could beat the information out of him. And as I beat him, I told him the truth — that the boy in the fire was your boyfriend. I shouted at him that it was Milo, not Freddy who died in that fire. *It was Milo!*"

The words echoed in Declan's head. Archie's last words — "*Tell Hunt, it was Milo.*"

Tom's face was crimson and he was panting.

Freddy laughed. "You know, there was a time when I could have learned to love my father, but we didn't exactly part on good terms. And it might surprise you to find out that I saw you that day, the day you visited my dad last week. I was there parked on the street. I wasn't a hundred percent sure before, but now I know it was you. You're going to pay for what you've done."

Declan saw movement out of the corner of his eye. Simon had pulled a gun out of his pocket. He aimed it at Freddy. Declan lunged forward and knocked Freddy to the ground as the gun went off. Everything went into slow motion. With Freddy on the floor, there was nothing to stop the bullet from passing directly from Simon's gun into Tom's chest. At almost the same time, Charlie leapt toward the couch, knocking the gun from Simon's hand.

Declan quickly rose, reached into his bag then retrieved the pair of handcuffs he had taken with him to Jasper. He grabbed a hold of Simon and got his arms behind his back, securing them with the cuffs. Then he ran to Tom, who was bleeding profusely. His eyes were closed, and he had lost consciousness. The bullet had done its work, and it was clear he wasn't going to make it.

Declan yelled to Freddy, "Give me your fucking gun!"

Freddy did as he was told, then calmly asked, "What do we do now?"

Declan pulled out his phone. "We call the police."

* * * *

The Paddock was a hive of activity. The forensics team removed Tom's lifeless body. Simon had been taken into custody by the RCMP. The police had just finished taking statements from Declan, Charlie and Freddy, when a familiar face entered the living room. Gary Sawchuck walked over to Declan, punched him gently on the shoulder and said, "Everywhere you go, you stir up trouble, don't you?"

Declan shrugged. "I guess I lead a charmed life."

"You may not even realise it, but you and your sidekick over there have helped us track down quite a bit of illegal activity."

"I know."

"I don't think you realise the full extent of it, though," Sawchuck said.

Declan tilted his head, "All right. Enlighten me."

"Well, for starters, I know you said that Tom confessed to Archie Whitcher's murder, but we can't prove he did it without more evidence. Fortunately there was a gun in his room with fingerprints all over it. And if we get a match on the bullet in Archie's body, that will ensure that Archie's death is accounted for."

Declan nodded. "I'm sure he did it. And I'm sure he killed Milo Griffin, too."

"Well, that one's a little harder to prove ten years on, but one thing is for sure — with the evidence you found, we know that Freddy Whitcher *is* who he says he is. Even if the picture and his testimony weren't enough, DNA will confirm Freddy is Archie Whitcher's son. And there's one other death we think we might be able to attribute to Tom Semple."

Declan raised his eyebrows in surprise. "Oh?"

"Freddy told you he got in touch with Harlen Feist with proof that Simon had arranged to have his son killed. It turns out Mr Feist was dying in hospital, but took a sudden, suspicious downturn. On the afternoon of his death, he was visited by a man matching Tom Semple's description. The nurses recalled a guy in a camelhair coat with a fedora, a scarf around his face, and sunglasses. Funny thing, we found all of those items in Tom's room."

"So, what'll happen to Simon Griffin?"

Sawchuck smiled. "Another piece of good luck. Freddy made more than one copy of the USB key with the recording of Simon's illegal dealings. Would you believe one arrived on my desk today? Freddy said that when he saw my name attached to the investigation of the death of his father in Calgary, he decided I was the one he should send the information to. A full circle moment. But that's not all. We did a survey of the house here, and you're not going to believe what we found in Simon's office."

"Another dead body?"

"Not directly, but there are human remains."

"What the hell?"

Gary continued, "There's a vault in Simon's office that not only has the antiquity mentioned in the conversation on the USB key, but a whole bunch of other items, including bones and mummified remains. Altogether, they're worth millions. And what's more, it would appear that none of them are legal for a private collector to have. Between ordering the hit on Harlen Feist's son, the shooting of Tom Semple and a range of charges connected to illegal possession of stolen goods, Simon Griffin is going away for a long time. So when we get back to Calgary, I owe you a drink."

A woman Declan had never seen before entered the room. She was accompanied by a police officer who was clearly letting her know what had happened over the past few hours in the house. Her face betrayed little emotion, but Declan noted that her hands were shaking.

Charlie walked over to her. "Jasmine. Are you all right?"

Declan realised that this must be the housekeeper Charlie had told him about. He made his way over to her. "I'm Declan Hunt. Charlie here says you were very helpful during his investigation. I'm so sorry you had to come home to all of this."

Jasmine smiled weakly. "It's quite a shock...to find out Milo is truly dead, and to have Mr Semple shot by Mr Griffin... It's hard to believe."

Declan put his hand gently on her shoulder. "If you need any help at all..."

Jasmine pursed her lips. "Thanks. I'll be fine." She slowly surveyed the room. "I think I need a cup of tea." She turned toward Charlie and Declan. "Would you care to join me?"

"That would be nice," Declan replied nodding at Charlie.

Jasmine led them into the kitchen where she steeped a pot of tea and poured it into three mugs. She sat at the table in silence, then said. "Do you believe in fate, Mr Hunt?"

Declan paused. "Why do you ask?"

Jasmine continued, "Looking at all of this, it just reminds me that none of us are really in control of our destiny. I saw an exhibit of sculptures last year made up of scraps of funnels, and bicycle wheels, sewing machines and dolls. Usually the doll was at the centre with its hands on a crank, and at first glance it seemed that when it turned that crank, the world around it started to spin. But that's not how it really worked. No matter how it appeared, that little doll wasn't making that crank turn, the crank was keeping the doll working. Life's an illusion, Mr Hunt. I think we're all just serving something bigger that we never really understood in the first place."

She shook her head sadly, then took another sip of her tea.

Declan considered what she'd said and thought about the past ten years of his life. Maybe she was right.

Chapter Thirty-Four

Charlie sat in Declan's office. "So, I guess now that my missing persons case is solved, we need to find some more work."

Declan nodded. He had a far-off look in his eyes.

"You've been quiet all weekend. What are you thinking about?" Charlie asked.

Declan shifted in his chair. "I've been trying to decide if I'd rather not know the truth about the past. Finding out that Freddy was still alive, that was... I've lived the last ten years based on a lie. Imagine, Freddy pretending to be someone else all that time."

"I know a bit about that," Charlie replied. "For the last ten years I haven't exactly been honest about who *I* am, at least not with my parents."

Declan was silent for a moment. "I don't want to scare you, but if you've hidden things in the past, there's always a price to pay when the truth comes out. When my dad found out I was gay, a lot of things shifted, and not for the better. And Freddy...he paid a much bigger price. I can't even begin to imagine the effect it'll have on him for the rest of his life."

Charlie got up and moved over to Declan. "What Archie did was horrible, but in the end, his final thoughts were about Freddy. He used his last bit of strength to send a message to you so you could help him. I know that doesn't erase what Archie had done, but there's no way to go back and change the past. Maybe the best we can hope for is that by revealing the truth we open up the possibility for a better future."

"You're a wise man, Charlie Watts," Declan said, ruffling Charlie's hair.

"What do you think's going to happen to Freddy now?"

"I placed a called to Katherine O'Grady," Declan said. "Last time I saw her, she told me she was the executor of Archie's will. It seems to me that as his closest relative, Freddy may be entitled to the house, and if that's the case, he can sell it and use the money to start fresh. I doubt he'd want to live there. It must have a lot of bad memories."

There was a knock at the door and Mrs B walked into the office. "I hope I'm not interrupting. I just got a call from a woman named Jasmine Robertson. She wanted to pay the bill for Simon Griffin. I told her she could e-transfer the money. Funny thing, though, she said she was going to add a bonus of ten thousand dollars. I'm not sure whose money it is, but she said given the nature of the incident on Friday, she felt you were owed a little recompense for the danger her boss put you in. Exactly what *did* you get up to on Friday?"

"It's a long story, Mrs B," Charlie replied.

Declan grinned at Charlie. "Well, I suppose maybe now we can afford to build that office wall I promised you."

Charlie's phone rang. "Excuse me for just a minute. I have to take this."

He answered the call. A voice on the other end said, "Charlie, I need to see you. The birds have left the nest and won't be home until later this evening."

It was Gran. She was letting him know that his parents had gone out and it was safe to visit her.

"I'll be right over," Charlie said. He looked at Declan, "I mean...we'll be right over. There's someone I'd like you to meet."

* * * *

Declan and Charlie pulled up to the house. It had been over six months since Charlie had moved out, but he swore that the pine tree on the front yard looked taller.

Charlie led Declan to the side entrance. "Mom hates a snowy mess on the front hall carpet," he explained. He opened the door and called out, "Hey, Gran, it's me!"

His grandmother appeared at the top of the stairs. She seemed much older than when he'd last seen her in the hospital. The cast on her wrist didn't help. Charlie bounded up the steps and gave her a gentle hug. "I thought I was going to lose you."

She grinned. "It'd take more than a fall to do me in, Charlie-boy. Now, are you just going to leave that handsome man down on the landing, or are you going to introduce us?"

"Gran," Charlie started, then beckoned Declan to come upstairs. "Gran, this is Declan. He's..." Charlie stumbled on the words. "He's my boyfriend." He just managed to squeak out the last word.

"Come on up here and give me a hug."

Declan walked up the stairs and gently hugged her. "It's a pleasure to finally meet you."

"Come to the kitchen," she said. "You can make me a cup of tea."

Charlie looked at Declan and beamed. This was the first time he'd ever introduced a member of his family to a boyfriend. Not really surprising given that Declan was the only person he'd ever called 'boyfriend'. He'd taken the first step, and it felt right.

Time flew as Gran peppered Declan with questions about his work and how it compared to the detective shows on TV. They had been talking for about an hour when Charlie heard car doors slamming. He glanced out of the kitchen window.

"No. It can't be. They're home early. We have to go. Now!"

"Charlie," Gran said, "you don't have to run."

The side door opened.

"We're home, Mom," his dad called out. "The ring road is closed. Some idiot—"

He turned the corner, looked into the kitchen and saw Charlie and Declan. He stood at the door and stared.

"Mom, would you like a cup of tea?" Charlie's mother called out as she tried to get past his father. "Ted, you're in the..."

Charlie gave up hope that either he and Declan, or his parents would disappear.

"Mom. Dad. We just dropped by to see how Gran was doing."

Declan stood, extending his hand. "Mr and Mrs Watts, so nice to finally meet you. I'm Declan Hunt."

Ted Watts looked at Declan's hand for a moment, then shook it. Charlie took a deep breath.

"Charlie, it's so nice to see you!" his mother chirped out, running around the table to hug him. Charlie grabbed onto her.

"So...you're the one my son works for?" his dad asked Declan.

"Yes. He's changed the way the company works. His computer knowledge has dragged us into the modern age. I just don't know what I'd do without him, and now that he's just about ready to get his private investigator's licence, I can see him making full partner in the near future."

Ted folded his arms. "That sounds like a serious commitment. That's not what he went to university for."

"Maybe not, but Charlie's good at his job. I'll have you know," Declan continued, "that in the past week, your son has solved a cold case that's baffled the police for the past ten years, and then rescued a young man who had been in hiding for half his life. You should be very proud of him."

Ted Watts looked back and forth from Declan to Charlie.

"Declan is exaggerating my role in those cases just a little," Charlie said.

"Actually, I'm not. I don't even think your son knows how important he is in the running of the company. It's hard to admit, but until he came into my life, I was just stumbling along. You must know what that's like, Mr Watts — to not feel complete until you find that one person to make up everything that's missing in your life."

Charlie's mother tilted her head and her face flushed.

"I'm not sure exactly what you're saying," Ted replied as he started to take short, rapid breaths.

Now was the time to say what Charlie needed to say. "Dad… Declan and I are seeing each other…like a couple. That's because I'm gay."

Charlie's father said nothing. He appeared to be processing Charlie's words.

"Did you hear that, Ted?" Gran said. "They're dating. Isn't it nice that Charlie has a special friend, and one who runs his own business?"

Declan interjected. "I promise you — your son is one of the most important things in my life, and I'll make sure he doesn't get hurt."

"But what about Carrie?" Charlie's mom asked.

Gran shook her head. "Oh, for crying out loud, Maggie. She's always known he's gay and they're nothing more than good friends."

Charlie turned back toward his father. "Dad… I love him, and he loves me and I hope that you and Mom can accept us." Charlie reached out and took Declan's hand.

Ted walked out of the room, then left the house, got in the car and drove away. Charlie tried to fight back his tears.

"He'll be fine." Gran said. "He just needs time to think about things. It'll take him a while to come around, but I know him, and he will. He's never been good with change."

Charlie faced his mother. "Are you all right?"

She smiled, then pointed to Declan. "Well, at least you've got a good-looking boyfriend. I guess I always suspected that you were different, Charlie, and if this is who you are, and this is what you want, I'm behind you. I love you no matter what." She paused. "And let me deal with your father."

Charlie hugged his mother. "Well, we should be going. I promise I'll come back soon."

Declan and Charlie each kissed Maggie and Gran on the cheek, then made their way back to the car.

The drive home began in silence but eventually Declan said, "I really admire what you did back there. That took real courage. Watching you come out to your folks like that, that got me thinking…"

They pulled up to a stoplight. Declan looked at Charlie and asked, "Do you think you might want to take this relationship to the next level and maybe move in with me full-time? I think I'm ready to commit…one hundred percent."

Charlie turned to Declan and kissed him full on the lips, then replied, "Yes!"

Chapter Thirty-Five

Charlie woke up snuggled into Declan. His face was buried in Declan's hair. He took a deep breath. *You smell like my boyfriend.* He lay there, soaking up the warmth of the man's body. At this moment, he had everything he needed…except for coffee. He carefully got out of bed and made his way down to the office. The sun hadn't come up yet. He wondered what time it was, but his eyes were too blurry to read the clock.

He went to the kitchenette, grabbed the espresso machine's reservoir and took it into the staff washroom to fill it with water. When he stepped back out, Dave the dead barista was waiting for him near the coffee maker. Charlie had come to accept that the office was haunted and that Dave wasn't a threat.

"Cortado, right?" Dave asked.

"You got it," Charlie replied.

In a minute, Dave presented him with a steaming hot coffee. He smiled as much as his partially burnt face allowed. "Well, I guess my job here is finished."

Dave started to shimmer, then he began to change. He got smaller and younger until the person facing Charlie looked a lot like the young Milo from the picture Simon Griffin had given him.

"Thank you. Thank you for everything," the ghost said before fading into nothing.

Charlie drank his coffee, then made his way back up the stairs and crawled into bed with Declan.

It seemed like only a second later that Charlie woke again. This time everything was clearer. The encounter with Dave had obviously been a dream. Charlie smiled. It was the gentlest dream he had experienced, and this one had been positive. Then an eerie whisper drifted through the room. "*Thank you for everything.*" A chill ran down his spine. As he dove under the sheets, he heard the sound of coffee being poured into a mug.

Dave?

"Good morning, sleepyhead."

Charlie peered out from beneath the covers. Declan walked toward him and handed him a cup of coffee. "What's wrong? You look spooked?"

"I had a weird dream again last night," Charlie said. He sat up in the bed. "Have you seen or heard anything odd around here?"

"Odd? Like what?"

Charlie took a sip from his cup. "Ghosts?" he said tentatively.

Declan smiled. "Noooooo," he answered. "Why?"

"Well... I've seen some things that...well, I can't explain. Or I couldn't until Gwen told me the history of this place."

"What history?"

"Didn't you know? It used to be a funeral home when it was built. God knows how many dead bodies have seen the inside of this building."

"W-wait a minute. Gwen told you that?"

"Yeah. It's carved into the stonework right above the doors. 'Hallowell Brothers, Undertakers'."

Declan burst out laughing. "Charlie, have you been worrying about this for long?"

"Well, worrying might be a bit dramatic, but, like I said, a lot of weird things have been going on. At first I thought I was just stressed out because of the case."

"Well, you can relax, Charlie. The case is closed, and there's never been a funeral home here."

"But the carving above the door…?" he asked, shaking his head.

Declan got into bed beside him. "Gwen's sign covers the last part of the carving, right?"

Charlie nodded.

"What it says is 'Hallowell Brothers, Under*writers*'… They were an insurance company."

"But Gwen said…"

"I'll have to have a little chat with her when I see her later."

Charlie frowned. "You mean…Gwen *lied* to me?"

"I think she was just putting you on."

"No. She lied. Plain and simple."

"Simple. Just like the guy who believed—" Declan started.

"If you're smart, mister, you will *not* finish that sentence."

Declan set down his coffee. "Why don't I help you take your mind off ghosts?" He rolled on top of Charlie and started to nibble on his neck. "I doubt your ghosts can measure up to what I'm about to do to you."

* * * *

Jasmine Robertson reclined in Simon's large leather chair in the sun room of The Paddock. She never tired of the view from this vantage point, especially in the morning as the sun rose above Sundance Ridge, which spread out before her beyond the Bow River.

This morning she was at peace. Jasmine had arranged for Declan Hunt Investigations to be well paid for their work because they had helped her more than she'd ever thought possible — so many loose threads taken care of all at once. Simon was in jail, Tom was dead, Harlen Feist was gone and, at a special meeting held last night, Jasmine had been appointed as the head of Monarch Holdings. Very few people in the organisation knew about the power she held. Jasmine was not just 'the housekeeper' — she was a clever strategist hiding in plain sight.

The police had taken away all of Simon's ill-gotten gains from the vault. Jasmine had conveniently opened it during a private moment when the police weren't in Simon's office, but they hadn't done a very thorough search of the rest of the house. They certainly hadn't found the smaller vault behind the wall in Jasmine's clothes closet — a vault that contained money, jewels, weapons and numerous documents that had information on people which would keep them from questioning her position. While the world might be a machine that often exerted its power on its players, Jasmine had made a choice not to let fate control her. She was the architect of her own universe. And now that she had control, she had some ideas about a few things she wanted to take care of in the near future…things that would involve two men by the names of Declan Hunt and Charlie Watts.

Sign up for our newsletter and find out about all our romance book releases, eBook sales and promotions, sneak peeks and FREE romance books!

Want to see more from this author?
Here's a taster for you to enjoy!

The Woodcarver's Model
Peter E. Fenton

Excerpt

He closed the door behind him and leaned against it as if his weight would hold out the world. How many of them had there been? When was he going to learn to think before he acted? This time he could have died. His heart raced. Fucking idiot! Where the fuck had Yussuf gone?

Rob woke with a start. From the look on the face of the passenger in seat 2B, Rob must have gasped or yelled. He was breathing heavily. Rob pressed the call button for the flight attendant. There was time for one more gin and tonic before they landed.

Once in the airport, after passing through customs, he retrieved his luggage from the baggage carousel. One large green canvas duffle bag — which looked more like it had been dragged by the plane rather than stored in its cargo hold — was all he had, other than his beaten-up leather shoulder bag. He made it out to the cab stand and took the next available taxi.

"Queen's Quay Terminal building, please," he said to the driver, then closed his eyes. He didn't want to appear to be rude by not talking. *So Canadian*, he thought. The *oh-look-I've-fallen-asleep* ruse usually fended off any attempt at mindless chatter from a driver. And he didn't need to see the sights. The ride from Toronto's Pearson International Airport to his home on the lake shore was nothing to see. It was all highway, industrial complexes, stubby office buildings and shopping malls. The trip showed Toronto as the ugly, unimaginative metropolis that it was, until they hit the expressway by the lake. Then it all changed — the lake, so big that it looked like a sea, the gaudy glamour of the Palais Royale dance hall, and the century-old buildings of the Canadian National Exhibition — they still made Rob smile. A quick left onto Queen's Quay and he was almost home.

During the cab ride, he thought of his last night in Mogadishu. Of returning to his hotel room after dinner with his photographer. The Hotel Mustaqbal on the traffic-jammed Wadada Uganda was one of the better accommodations in this war-torn country. Clean rooms with a fair certainty of hot and cold running water. What else could he have asked for in Somalia?

When he'd entered the room, he had sensed, without even turning on the lights, that everything had been tossed. He'd frozen, not wanting to make a sound in case the intruders were still there. Whoever'd done this was probably looking for his computer, jewellery, identity papers — anything of value. The joke was on them. He'd learned years ago never to travel with electronics, other than his phone, and he kept that and his identification on him at all times. And he wrote everything in notebooks. He never had to worry about notebooks. No one wanted them, they didn't break and they didn't run out of power in a jungle. He'd once lost his pen in Tierra del Fuego but was still able to finish writing using a charred stick from the fire.

As he had surveyed the damage in his hotel room, he'd heard a noise. Out of the corner of his eye, he'd seen a figure make for the window. It was Abdi, his driver. Abdi had thrown himself out the window onto the fire escape. Rob had chased him. Why? He didn't know.

They'd both hit the main street running. Rob had run right past a man leaning against a car talking to someone in front of the hotel. He'd kept going for another few hundred yards before realising it had been his guide, Yussuf. It was a few blocks later, on a small side street, that Abdi had yelled something in Somali to a few men. One had pulled out a gun and started firing at Rob. Rob had been pinned in a doorway, shards of concrete flying all around him, when he'd heard more shouting. More firing. *Where the fuck was Yussuf?* Then there was silence. Finally, a familiar head had poked around the corner.

"It's safe now, boss. You come. Come!" Yussuf had waved him to follow. In his hand, he'd held an old CAR-15 automatic rifle. A body lay in the street. Rob hadn't stopped to see who it was.

Life as an adventure travel writer was not what he thought it would be when he began this job. There was adventure, and there was this. One of these days, the adventure was going to win and all of the Yussufs in the world would not be able to save him.

* * * *

"Just by the water taxi stand, please."

The driver pulled over to the curb. Rob paid the fare, wished him a good day, then toted his bag over to the pier.

The water taxi was a small open boat that ferried passengers from the mainland to one of the Toronto Islands. Formed from sediment washed from the Scarborough Bluffs to the east, the islands had once been a large sandbar which extended as an unbroken spit into the waters of Lake Ontario. Hurricanes in the mid-1800s had severed what were now the islands from the mainland. Over the years, houses, some no more than holiday shacks, had cropped up. Larger homes had followed. SeaBreeze, a modest three-bedroom, two-storey house with a roof deck, had been built in the late 1960s by Rob's parents. They'd seen it as a needed quick-access get-away from their busy urban life. It was now the place Rob called home.

The sign for SeaBreeze, pegged to the front door, had been hand-carved by a local craftsman who'd missed the space after the *Sea*. Rob's parents had found it charming and wouldn't let him re-carve it. Here, Rob was at peace. It was just him, the trees and Lake Ontario. The sounds of waves on the shore and the cries of the birds were the only music he needed. They reminded him of his parents, and they were good memories.

He walked through the front door and everything was as he'd left it. All except for the dishes in the sink and the black bra on the floor under the baby grand piano. He was fine with that. At least, he would be fine with it as soon as he tidied everything up. And as soon as he'd settled in, he would call his cleaner to book an appointment.

As much as Rob thrived on chaos in the field, home had to be...organised. It was his problem, he realised that, but this was his home. Karen, who took care of the place when he was on assignment, was, to put it politely, a slob. *"Look after your house? Of course I don't mind. Why would I? You've seen where I live. Looking after a flophouse would be a step up in the world."* It was because of Karen that he'd bought the piano. He couldn't play a note. It had to be tuned regularly because of the lakefront humidity, but that didn't matter because Karen loved it, and she could play like Billy Joel.

Anyone seeing this house and hearing that the owner was a travel writer might think that writing was quite a profitable venture. SeaBreeze, with its luxurious finishes and lake view, could lead them to that conclusion, but they'd be wrong. Rob Hanson made little money. Some years not enough to cover expenses. This lifestyle was thanks to his parents — structural engineers who'd specialised in large-scale hydroelectric projects. They'd flown down to inspect one of their constructions on the Marañón River in Peru when their plane had gone down. That was twenty years ago.

Rob felt that he'd had a happy childhood. His parents had been his best friends. They'd treated him like an adult from an early age, openly discussing their lives, sharing their fascinations and friends with him. He had always felt safe, comfortable and loved.

He'd been raised by his parents in an old Victorian house on South Drive, in Toronto's Rosedale neighbourhood, one of the city's wealthiest communities. It was the home of the old-time gentry — of merchants, doctors and lawyers, of inheritors of money that no longer seemed to work for a living. The other two most affluent neighbourhoods, Forest Hill and the Bridle Path, were built for a different sort, each with its own...requirements. Rosedale, for instance, was the realm of the old white Anglo-Saxon Protestants. Rumour had it that even during the latter part of the last century, people couldn't purchase there if they were Jewish. The wealthy and well-connected Jews and foreign émigrés established themselves in Forest Hill, an enclave of newer stately homes constructed a little further from the centre of their world — Toronto. The third neighbourhood, the Bridle Path, was for the gaudy nouveau riche — entertainers and entrepreneurial magnates — who desired large mansions and larger properties still within the confines of the metropolis.

Homes on South Drive, like their owners, were on the modest side of wealth. Rob's parents had been accepted there despite their lack of historic connections, by virtue of being *clever people*. A neighbourhood like Rosedale liked clever people. It wore them like a Hermès scarf. Clever people made the other people feel chic and intelligent.

What Rob loved most about South Drive was its proximity to the Moore Park Ravine, a large expanse of wilderness in the city. He'd spent most of his free time there, exploring, making trails even deeper into his own private jungle. Here, his imagination had run wild. Here, he had learned the names of every tree, shrub, animal and fungus. Here, he had taught himself how to photograph everything from the largest tree to the smallest insect. But, more importantly, he'd learned to love, respect and understand nature.

Rob had been in his mid-twenties when he'd heard the news that his parents had gone missing. Their plane had gone down in the Peruvian jungle. When he'd received the news from an old family friend, a company lawyer, there'd been a bit of a disconnect. He'd heard the words, but his mind had only focused on Peru. *That's where Paddington Bear came from. Deepest, darkest Peru. I wonder if they'll meet any bears?* Why a twenty-five-year-old would have that thought had never occurred to him at the time.

He had been flown down to the area by his parents' company during the search. Karen, whom he'd known since university days, had come along for support.

Rob's sister, Jessica, thought too young to be involved, had been left in the care of their aunt.

It had taken authorities three weeks to discover the tangled wreckage of his parents' DHC-7. Rob had held Karen's hand as they were flown to the crash site by helicopter. There'd been no sign of human remains left at the site. He and Karen hadn't spoken. They'd clasped hands and focused on breathing. Neither had experienced death up until then.

As he'd stood in the jungle, surrounded by shards of debris, Rob had cried. He'd thought of never seeing his parents again, not knowing if they got out of the plane in time and were still out there...lost. Or had the animals... No, he wouldn't let his mind wander there. But the more he had looked around, the more he'd felt, as inappropriate as it might have seemed, that in some strange way, his parents would have liked this as their final resting place. They'd both loved the wilderness. Rob had stayed on-site for the following week as the search continued, and the longer he stayed, the more peace he'd found. It was there that he had discovered what he wanted to do with his life — explore the wilderness.

When his parents' estate had been settled, including the sale of their company, Rob Hanson discovered that he would never have to fear for his financial future. He'd become one of Toronto's most eligible bachelors.

About the Author

The Burnt marks Peter E. Fenton's fourth novel with Entwined Publishing. It is the third book in the Declan Hunt Mysteries series.

Peter's first book, *The Woodcarver's Model*, came out in April of 2022 and was a four-time nominee in the Goodreads M/M Romance Readers' Choice Awards. The other two books in the Declan Hunt Mysteries series are *Mann Hunt*, which was nominated for a Goodreads M/M Romance Readers' Choice Award and recently released in Spanish; and *Hoodoo House*, which was also a Goodreads M/M Romance Readers' Choice Award nominee, and released in Spanish as *Casa Hoodoo*.

Peter is also a playwright who has penned the book for four musicals — *The Giant's Garden*, *Newfoundland Mary*, *Bemused*, and *The Detective Disappears* — which have had professional productions across Canada and the USA. He spent many years working in palaeontology in remote locations including the Canadian Rockies, the Northwest Territories and Nunavut. Peter currently resides in Toronto, Canada, with his partner of over twenty years. At heart, he is an incredible romantic.

Peter loves to hear from readers. You can find his contact information, website details and author profile page at https://www.firstforromance.com

ENTWINED PUBLISHING